With Spink & Son's

respectful Compliments

S LITTLE
LECTION
_____

-20

LDER

5, 6 & 7, King Street,
St James's,
London, SW1Y 6QS

CONTENTS

COURAGEOUS BIKER DADDY	1
WILD BIKER DADDY	53
VIGOROUS BIKER DADDY	103
CARNAL BIKER DADDY	155
LOVING BIKER DADDY	207

Copyright © 2022 by Scott Wylder
All rights reserved.

http://www.scottwylderauthor.com/

In no way is it legal to reproduce, duplicate, or transmit any part of this document in either electronic means or in printed format. Recording of this publication is strictly prohibited, and any storage of this document is not allowed unless with written permission from the publisher. All rights reserved.

Get your FREE BOOK and much more being part of Reader's group

COURAGEOUS BIKER DADDY

1

Bethany

"Come on, ladies, enough beauty sleep for you." A biker banged on the door. "Get your asses presentable and out here in 10 minutes."

I whimpered and got to my feet, wincing. I felt so sore from being used. I didn't know how long it had been since I was kidnapped by a member of the Demon biker gang and brought to work in the Pleasure Room. I lost count of the days. Enough time had passed where I didn't try to escape anymore. Not that there was anything for me to escape to.

Now I slept in a room with about a dozen or so other women. I smoothed out my hair and the lacy red dress I was wearing. If I didn't look presentable, then I would be in trouble.

Right now I didn't care about anything except not making them angry.

We got ready in silence. We didn't talk much to each other. There was never enough energy at the end of the day to form a connection.

The biker pounded on the door again. "Hurry up!"

We filed out of the room and lined up. The biker-- I think his name was Reaper-- sized us up. He stopped when he got to me and grinned. "Smile for me, honey."

I forced a smile. He grabbed my chin and forced me to look up at him. "You'll pass enough," he said. "Stop looking so glum. You're supposed to be enjoying yourself."

Right. I had to act like I was willing.

I followed the others into the Pleasure Room. It looked like an actual nightclub with music playing, dim lighting, and even a bar in one corner. Black leather couches separated by curtains lined the walls.

There were a few Demons who stood at attention to make sure we behaved ourselves. But there were only a few men in the place because it was still early.

I started to dance on the dancefloor as if I really was at a club. As if I was just a carefree woman having fun.

I didn't know what that felt like, but I guess I pretended well enough.

If I was lucky it would be a slow night and I could spend most of it dancing. Maybe the men wouldn't see me. Maybe they would take other girls back to the couches.

A girl could dream, right?

Someone grabbed my hand and my heart sank. I pasted a smile on my face and turned to look at the hulking man behind me. Fear sliced through me at the sight of him. He was huge, at least a foot taller than me. And even though he was wearing a white button-down shirt, I could see the muscles bulging out from under it. Shit. I hoped he was more gentle than he looked. I was already sore down there. "Hello, sir," I said. "Looking for some company tonight?"

"What's you're name?"

"Bethany," I said.

He smiled down at me. "Let's go talk somewhere private," he said.

I swallowed. Straight to business. Sometimes men would buy us drinks first. It made it easier to act like I enjoyed it when I was a bit intoxicated. No luck here.

I led him to one of the couches and closed the curtains so we could be alone. "Sit down and relax," I said as I started to take off my dress.

His hands grabbed mine. "That won't be necessary," he said. "I'm not here to hurt you."

I looked up at him, confused. He wasn't smiling anymore. His face was unreadable but I could see the tension in his shoulders. "S-sir?"

"My name is Ryker. I'm with the Hell's Renegades motorcycle club. I'm here to get you and all the other women in this place out."

I shook my head slowly. No way. This was too good to be true. This had to be a trap of some sort. "I-I don't know what you mean. I'm just here to have fun, sir."

"Bullshit."

I winced a little at his tone and his gaze softened slightly.

"Look," he said. "I don't want to scare you, but I don't have the time right now. I'm going to get you out of here, but you have to talk to me. How many other women are here? Are there any in the sleeping area or anywhere else? Or are they all in the Pleasure Room?"

I bit my lip. "If you're really here to try to save everyone, then you have to get out of here. The Demons are no joke. They'll kill you."

Ryker smirked. "Trust me, we've gone toe to toe with the Demons before. We can handle ourselves just fine. As long as you do everything I tell you to, I'll get you out of here alive. Okay?"

I wanted to believe him. I really did. But it seemed too good to be true. However, for the first time since I was trapped here, it felt like I had a real shot of getting out of here. "Okay," I said finally. "As far as I know, all the women are in here. There are Demons watching us and security cameras trained on us as well.

Ryker nodded. "Okay. That's all I needed to know. Thank you." He smiled at me kindly and grabbed my hand. "It's going to be okay, Bethany. You're safe now.:

2

Ryker

I pulled out my phone and sent a quick text to Chase, giving him the all clear. Then I led Bethany onto the dancefloor. I looked around, making note of the guards as well as the couches that had the curtains drawn for privacy. There were only a couple of them, luckily.

"Stay close to me," I told Bethany.

"Yes, sir."

I winced a little. I knew they were trained to call all the men sir but I hated it. It sounded too formal to me. I much preferred Daddy.

Of course, I also preferred my leather jacket to the button-down shirt I was wearing now, but I wouldn't have gotten in wearing club colors.

Suddenly the power was cut and everything fell silent aside from a few people murmuring and the sickening sounds of two people fucking on one of the couches. Then there was an explosion in the back of the building and the guards started shouting and running out the back. I made my way to the back door of the Pleasure Room and leaned on it so the Demons couldn't get back in if they tried. I put my arms around Bethany, holding her close to me. Then a shot rang out through the crowd and people screamed. Bethany whimpered next to me.

"It's okay," I whispered. "That's just Chase taking out the remaining guards in here. Don't worry."

She trembled in my arms. I wished I could make her feel better and take away her fear, but I knew that was impossible. Why the hell would she trust me after what the Demons did to her?

The doors to the outside opened just as the power came on. Chase came in along with Dean and Blaine. They kept the doors open and started to usher women outside. Dean tore open a closed curtain to reveal a naked woman with a man on top of her on the couch. He pulled the man off and started beating him.

"Take it easy, Dean," Blaine said as he handed the woman his jacket to keep her warm. "The guests aren't supposed to know it's a brothel. He probably thought it was just a consensual sex club."

Dean scowled. "Anyone with eyes could tell it was a brothel," he said.

Chase looked over at me and Bethany. "Are you good, Ryker?" he asked. He looked at Bethany. "Is she injured?"

I realized I hadn't moved. I had just stood in the back holding Bethany while they did all the work. "No," I said. I reluctantly let go of her. It was wrong, but holding her had felt so good. I did it only to make sure I didn't lose her in the crowd, but now I wanted to hold her again. It had felt so good. "We're good."

Chase jerked his head to the door. "Then let's go. We need to get them all out of here."

We all ran to the door. Outside were a couple of rented minivans driven by club members. Dean and Blaine were helping women inside. Bethany stopped walking beside me. Her eyes were wide with terror as she looked at the scene.

One of the women was panicking and she tried to run into the forest. Chase grabbed her arm before she got far. He looked up at me. "Get her!" he shouted.

I turned to look and realized Bethany was gone, sprinting off into the forest.

"Shit," I muttered.

I took off after her. Despite being half-starved and tortured every day for god knew how long, she was fast. I had to chase her through the woods, past where Chase had stashed his bike and mine. Finally, she tripped over a rock and fell to the ground. She backed up away from me, trembling.

"Easy," I said. I kept my hands up so she would see everything was okay. "I told you before, I'm not going to hurt you."

She shook her head. "You were forcing them into vans," she said. "You're just going to use me like the Demons did."

I grimaced. I didn't blame her for thinking that. That's

exactly what it looked like. "No," I said. "I'm not going to do that, I promise. You're safe with me."

She glared at me as she picked herself up. I could tell she was about to bolt again. I grabbed her, wrapping my arms around her.

"Let go of me!" She tried to kick me and struggle, but I held firm.

"Would you listen to me?" I shouted. "You won't make it anywhere on foot. We're trying to get you to safety. If you keep running, the Demons are going to find you and they're going to kill you."

"You don't know that!"

"Yes, I do." I turned her around to face me, keeping a firm grip on her arms. "Look, you're fast and you're smart. But they have motorcycles and they won't risk anyone escaping just in case you find a cop or reporter that isn't in their pocket. You're only chance is coming with me."

She shook her head. "I don't believe you."

"You don't have to." I started dragging her back. It was hard to keep a firm grip on her without hurting her. But I needed to get her out of here. It was the only chance at safety.

By the time we reached the bikes, Chase was already there. "The vans have already left with Blaine and Dean," he said. "They couldn't wait. Demons were already starting to get out of the building."

I nodded. I had figured as much. "I have Bethany who will comply. Won't you?" I grabbed her arm a little tighter and she whimpered. Guilt stabbed through me but I held firm. She could be scared of me and she could hate me, but at least she wouldn't end up with a bullet to the head.

Chase shook his head, his face grim. He hated it when we had to act like brutes as well. "I'll stay back and try to lure them away from you two. But you two will stick out like sore thumbs. Go to the Black Hawk bar and lay low for a while."

I nodded. "Be careful, okay?"

He grinned. "Don't worry. The Demons are still lousy shots. I'll be fine. Just get her to safety."

I grabbed my bike helmet and handed it to Bethany. "Put this on," I said.

She glared at me and didn't move.

"Look, you can either put it on and come willingly, or I'll force the helmet on and tie you to my bike, "I growled. "Either way, you're leaving with me."

For a moment her lips trembled. Despite her brave face, she was on the verge of tears. But she put the helmet on and got on my bike.

I got on in front of her and felt her wrap her arms around my waist and I sped out of the woods and to the main road.

3

Bethany

I had been hoping Ryker would bike at a slower speed so I could tuck and roll away and try to escape again. But that wasn't possible. Even through the forest, we were going fast. Branches whipped at my arms and legs as we went through the forest, headed towards the main road. I was grateful I had the helmet at least to protect me from that. I couldn't imagine how Ryker was feeling with the branches hitting his face directly.

His partner had disappeared. He had said something about distracting the Demons while Ryker got me to "safety". I didn't believe he was taking me to safety. Not after I watched his partner force that woman into the van.

I didn't know what sort of turf war had started between his group and the Demons, but it looked like the other women and I were caught in the crossfire.

It had been stupid of me to trust him. When did

someone just show up out of the middle of nowhere to help? It just didn't happen.

We reached the main road and I couldn't help but feel a little relieved. At least I wasn't getting hit by branches.

And then I heard the roar of a motorcycle behind us and a shot fired, going past my ear. Ryker swerved suddenly and then went down a dirt road. I was barely able to hold on. I heard them following us but Ryker biked even faster, taking another turn and then another through winding dirt roads. Finally, he stopped.

I felt dizzy and a little nauseous from all of the turns, despite my empty stomach and I pulled off the helmet, gulping in the fresh air. I couldn't have outrun Ryker even if I tried. But he grabbed my arm anyway, keeping me close as he dragged me and the bike into the forest, off the road. Once the road was out of sight, he lied the bike on the ground. He let go of my arm to cover the bike with leaves. I tried to muster up some strength to get away, but I was only able to stumble back a little before he grabbed me again.

With one smooth motion, Ryker swept my legs out from under me and I fell towards the ground. He wrapped his arms around me to break my fall at the last second. He pinned me to the ground with his body and his hand covered my mouth. Terror seized me and I tried to struggle. "Stay quiet," he breathed into my ear.

I knew it was fruitless. There's no way I could get away from him. He was so much stronger than me and even though he wasn't armed, he could snap me like a twig if I even tried. I had just gone from one captor to another.

My eyes felt hot and I bit back a sob as tears ran down my cheeks. Great. Now I was crying in front of him too. Showing him how weak I was.

If Ryker noticed, he didn't let on. He was focused on the sounds from the road.

Motorcycles roared in the distance before the sound faded away. Ryker waited for several long minutes, listening, before he turned his attention to me.

His brow furrowed as he looked at me before slowly taking his hand off my mouth. "I think we lost them," he said. He wiped my tears away with his thumb His touch was surprisingly gentle. "I know you don't trust me. And I don't blame you. But I swear I wouldn't have been so rough if I thought there was any other way."

I looked away from him, instead focusing on the dead leaves. I felt exhausted. All of the fight had gone out of me. "I'll be good, sir," I said. "I'll behave. Just please get off me."

He quickly got off me, kneeling next to me on the ground. He looked disheveled now. His white shirt was covered in dirt and sweat and there was a cut on one of his eyes. I had a feeling that was where a branch had hit him during our mad dash through the woods. But he didn't seem to care. Instead, he was looking me up and down. "Are you hurt?" he asked.

I shook my head. I was a little scraped up, but I wasn't in any real pain. I looked down at my skimpy dress and grimaced. It was ripped and dirty now. I was barely decent. And it wasn't doing anything to protect me from the stiff breeze that was picking up. I shivered a little.

Ryker started to unbutton his shirt and I tensed up. I

knew him using me was inevitable but I had hoped it would wait until we were inside first. I whimpered a little but I resisted the urge to try to run. He would just catch me again and this time he might not be so merciful.

He took off the shirt, revealing bulging muscles underneath it, as well as a tangle of tattoos on his arms and chest. I couldn't make out all of them, but I could clearly see an insignia right above his heart. That must be the insignia of his club.

He reached out to me and I flinched away before I realized his shirt was in his hand. He was giving it to me. "It's not much," he said. "And it's pretty dirty now. But it'll keep you a little warmer than that lace. I'll get you some real clothes as soon as I can."

I swallowed and took the shirt gratefully. His body heat still clung to it and despite the situation, it felt good. "Thank you, sir," I said as I wrapped the shirt around my shoulders.

"Another thing," he said. "Don't call me sir."

4

Ryker

I felt like an absolute monster. Even as we stood up and I unburied my bike, visions of pinning her down while she silently cried underneath me swam through my head. That was going to haunt me for awhile, if not the rest of my life.

I was a scary guy. I knew that. I've made grown men piss themselves before. But having a woman scared of me twisted like a knife in my stomach.

And the worst part was, she had good reason to be scared. I hadn't been gentle with her. I had forced her to come with me, even threatened her to make her comply. Why the fuck would she believe me when I told her I wouldn't hurt her?

At least she didn't seem willing to run anymore. Not because she suddenly trusted me. My guess was she was just exhausted. She had been through hell, after all. And I hadn't helped.

I sighed. "My plan was to take you to the Black Hawk bar, but it's too far away now. And they'll be staking the place out in case we show up. But there's a motel and truck stop not far from here. We'll go there. And then you can have a hot shower and some food."

She nodded. "Yes, s-- um... what should I call you?" She flinched, as if she expected me to hit her for asking a question.

"Call me Ryker," I said. I grabbed the helmet that had been abandoned on the ground next to the bike. I handed it to her and watched her put it on. "I'll go slower this time now that we lost the Demons. But hold on tight, okay?"

She nodded. "Yes, Ryker."

I got onto the bike and she got on behind me and wrapped her arms around my waist.

Luckily, the motel wasn't far away, only about a twenty minute bike ride. Which was good. The sooner Bethany could have some food and a hot shower, the better.

It was freezing outside now that it was getting even later in the day. The cold had sunk into my bones. I couldn't imagine how she was feeling in what little clothes she had.

I wished I had more to give her than a flimsy shirt. My leather jacket would have kept her warmer and it would have provided more protection if she fell off the bike.

When we rocked up to the motel, the sun had set. It was a shady establishment on the main road that didn't ask too many questions. But it was attached to a truck stop which would have food and maybe even some clothes.

I parked the bike behind the building, just in case the Demons kept up their search. "I'm going to get us a room," I said. "Look at me, Bethany."

She tilted her head up to look at me. I could barely make out her face through the visor. "You told me you would behave, didn't you?"

She nodded.

"If you try to run or hide, I'll find you and there will be consequences. Understand?"

She nodded again, this time more rapidly.

"Good girl."

The threat was empty, but she didn't have to know that.

I went to the check-in desk and got a room for the night as fast as I could. Luckily, this wasn't the sort of place to ask questions.

When I came back, Bethany was still sitting on the bike. I felt relieved. I wasn't up for chasing her again.

"Come on," I ordered. I held up the room key.

She followed me obediently to our room.

Once inside, I turned on the light, revealing one full-sized bed, a small nightstand, and not much else. It was all decorated in a dingy green. It looked pathetic.

But at least it was warm and had running water and a bed. I looked to see Bethany staring at the bed in absolute terror. My chest tightened. I wished there was something I could say to convince her I wouldn't force myself on her. But the words wouldn't come. I wasn't used to comforting someone. That had never been my job before. My job was usually beating someone's face in.

"I'm going to find some food and clothes," I said. "Make yourself comfortable. Take a shower. I won't be long."

"Thank you," she said. She took off my shirt and handed it to me. "Here."

I smiled. "Thank you, little one," I said.

I could have kicked myself for saying that. The name just slipped out.

Bethany gave no reaction to it. She was so tired, it might not have even registered.

I left the motel room and called Chase as I walked around the building to the truck stop. "Hey," I said.

"What's happening?" he asked. "I expected you to check in an hour ago."

"Change of plans," I said. "Demons tracked us down and

chased us away. We're currently holed up in a seedy motel for the night. I think I got them off our tail." I sighed as I entered the truck stop, which was part convenience store, part gift shop. "How are the others? Did you all get out okay?"

"Everything went according to plan on our end," Chase said. "I managed to lure a couple of the bikers away from you before losing them and regrouping with the others. Dean and Blaine are currently taking the women to a women's shelter right now."

"Good," I sighed. "That's good at least."

"You good?"

"Not really. I feel like shit. I don't think I can go on a raid again for a bit."

Chase whistled. "This one's really gotten to you, hasn't it?"

"I feel like an asshole. I am an asshole."

"Look, it sucks, I get it. But she would have died if you let her go."

"I know. I just wish I didn't have to wrestle her to the ground to make her comply. She's terrified of me. Maybe you or Diesel could come out here and take over."

"Do you think she would be less scared of us?"

He had me there.

"Look, this is a rough job for sure. But you need to get through it. Soon both of you will be safe. And then you can take a break. Just hold out for a little longer, okay?"

"Yeah," I muttered. "I will."

"Good. I've got to go, but keep me updated, all right?"

"I will. I'll bring her to Newbury in the morning, after things have calmed down some."

"Good plan."

After I hung up, I browsed through the store. I grabbed a baggy sweatshirt and pair of sweatpants, both emblazoned with the motel logo on them. They were roughly Bethany's size, or at least as close as I could get to Bethany's size. She was so small, they would still hang off of her.

The hot food section was limited. I wished I could get her something more nutritious, like soup or a homemade meal. But the best I could do was a couple of slices of pizza. At least it was warm and filling. I also bought a cup of hot tea which would hopefully help her relax a little.

In the checkout line, there was a section of teddy bears and other stuffies for truckers to bring home to their kids. On impulse, I grabbed one of the teddy bears. It was silly. I knew that. I didn't even know if she was a Little. And she definitely didn't see me as a Daddy.

But maybe it would give her a little bit of comfort anyway. God knew she needed it.

5

Bethany

While Ryker was gone, I took a shower. It felt so good being able to warm up and get clean. I hadn't realized how cold I was until I stepped into the hot water. It felt so good, I could stay in there forever.

I focused on getting clean as well as warming up. It felt nice to wash away all the dirt and sweat. I had scrapes on my elbows and knees, as well as a few scratches on my shoulder but I was lucky. No bruises or bleeding.

Honestly, Ryker had been pretty patient with me while I tried to escape. The Demons wouldn't have been so merciful if I had tried to escape them the first time, let alone the multiple times I tried to escape.

As I got out of the shower, I heard the door to the room open. I wrapped a towel around my body as I opened the door just in time to see Ryker come in. I swallowed, feeling tense and nervous. I was clean now and we weren't running from the Demons anymore. He could use me however he wanted.

But he barely glanced at me, instead putting a small pizza box on the nightstand. The smell of it made me ravenous. He set a cardboard cup next to it before holding out a plastic shopping bag. "Here," he said. "Clean clothes. I hope they fit."

I took the bag, noticing it was a little heavy. Relief filled me. Maybe he wasn't going to try to hurt me, at least not tonight.

Maybe I was wrong. Maybe I could trust him.

No. I couldn't think like that. I had to be prepared. He was still dangerous, even if he was showing me mercy right now.

I changed into the sweatshirt and sweatpants in the bathroom. They were definitely too big on me, but they were warm and cozy. Just wearing them made me feel more protected.

I went back out to see him setting up a makeshift bed on the floor with some pillows and blankets. I bit my lip as I watched him. Could I really be this lucky? Not only was he not planning on using me tonight, but he wasn't making me sleep with him at all. And he was even setting up a bed for me. I couldn't believe his generosity.

But I wondered why he would set it up in front of the door. Wasn't he worried I would escape?

He looked up at me after he finished setting up the bed. "I brought you pizza and hot tea," he said. "It's not a lot, but it was the best they had. I'll try to get you some real food soon."

It was more than enough. I couldn't even remember the last time I had pizza. We weren't allowed to eat much while we were in the Pleasure Room. Only enough to keep going. "Thank you," I said. "This is fantastic." I grabbed the pizza and sat down on the floor to eat. I groaned as soon as I took the first bite.

Ryker watched me while I ate. His expression was unreadable, but his brow was furrowed. He looked absolutely menacing.

I bit my lip as I froze. I realized he wasn't eating but there were two slices in the box. I slid the second slice over to him. "I'm sorry," I said. "I shouldn't have taken both slices."

He shook his head. "No, they're both for you."

"You're not eating?"

"Don't have an appetite tonight."

He still looked mad. I felt nervous asking him about it. He had already been so patient with me. I didn't want to press my luck. "D-did I do something wrong?" I hated the way my voice wobbled with nerves.

"Of course not," he said. "Why do you think that?"

I looked down at the pizza. "You look mad."

"I'm not angry at you, little one. I'm angry at myself. For scaring you and being so rough with you."

I frowned. Why would he be mad about that? It didn't make sense. "I-I'm okay, really. Just a few scratches. It's not like you hit me or anything."

He sighed. "I just wish I found another way."

I picked up my tea to take a sip. It was warm and relaxing. Peppermint. I smiled. I couldn't remember the last time I had hot tea. "It's okay. I'll be good. I won't try to run away anymore."

The answer didn't seem to satisfy him. He just ran his hand through his hair, looking frustrated. "You won't have to soon," he said. "Soon you'll be safe. You'll be away from me and you'll be safe."

I dashed that thought before it could let hope take route. I would never be safe. Even if Ryker stayed true to his word and got me out of reach of the Demons, I would just be on my own again. Homeless on the street. Sleeping in shelters and just trying to get by. Safety wasn't in my future.

"Is there anyone you want to call?" he asked. "Someone who might be worried about you being gone?"

I winced. It was as if he knew where my thoughts had gone. I shook my head. "No," I said. "There's no one. I didn't have anyone. I was just another homeless person on the streets, that's why it was so easy for the Demons to kidnap me."

He nodded. He didn't seem too surprised. "We'll take you to a battered women's shelter then. You'll be safe there."

I sighed. "I promise I won't run away," I said. "You've already proven to be nicer than the Demons. But please don't lie to me like this. I-I don't want to hope."

"I'm not lying," Ryker said. His voice was harsh. I looked up to see him looking determined. There was no sign of sarcasm or mocking. He just looked straight at me, matter of fact. "This was never about using you or the other women. It was about getting you to safety. The Hell's

Renegades aren't like the Demons. They don't hurt innocent people."

I wanted to believe him. I really did. But it was hard. "Why would you just risk your life by going up against the Demons?"

"Because it's worth it if we save people from them. Because I want to help people like you."

6

Ryker

It looked like she was finally believing me. It was finally sinking in that I didn't plan to force myself on her or hurt her. At least that's what I wanted to believe.

After she finished eating, she leaned against the side of the bed, looking exhausted. "We should get some sleep," I said as I lied down on the makeshift bed on the floor. "We're going to have a long day tomorrow."

"You're sleeping there?" She looked at me, looking genuinely surprised.

"Yes, little one."

She frowned, looking confused. She looked absolutely adorable when she was confused. I just wish it wasn't over someone showing her basic decency. "Won't you be more comfortable in the bed?" Bethany looked down, a slight blush coloring her cheeks. "I mean, I'm grateful. But I don't understand."

"You've been through hell," I said. "And I haven't exactly helped. So yes, you'll be sleeping on the bed. I won't disturb you. I promise."

She smiled and looked down, blushing. "Thank you," she said. "That's generous of you."

Fuck. I wanted to go and beat the shit out of everyone in her life. Because clearly she didn't know much kindness if she thought I was being generous. "Just sleep well, okay?"

She lied down on the bed, and then sat up. She was holding the little teddy bear. I forgot I had set it down on the bed. "Oh yeah," I said. "I got that in the store. It's a little silly, but I thought, I don't know, that it would give you a little comfort." I shrugged, trying to make it sound as if it was just an afterthought and no big deal. As if I wasn't coming very close to treating her like a Little.

She hugged the bear to her chest. "Thank you," she said. "I haven't had a stuffy since I was a little kid."

Fuck, she was adorable. I couldn't think about that. I couldn't think about how sweet she would be as a Little. She wasn't mine. She would never be mine.

I merely nodded in response and turned over onto my side. I listened as she got under the covers and turned off the light. Sweet dreams, little one.

The next morning I woke up to my phone ringing. I glanced up to see Bethany still asleep. I stood up and quietly stepped outside into the cold morning air. "Chase?"

"Change of plans," he said. "The Demons are staking us out. They have bikers set up all through the town."

I frowned. "Why all the manpower?" Surely by now they knew the women we rescued were long gone. Except for Bethany. But they didn't know that.

"I think they're after revenge," Chase said. I've called in reinforcements from the other presidents, but stay away from Newbury for at least another day."

I swore. "I just got her to start trusting me," I said. "If I tell her this, she might try to escape again."

"Then you're just going to have to keep catching her," he snapped. "Look, I'd love to talk more right now, but I can't. But Mac is on his way with a car. It'll be less conspicuous than your bike. Just get her away from Demon territory. But don't go near the women's shelter. The last thing we need is the Demons finding out where we send the women."

"Yeah," I said. "I'll do that."

After hanging up, I went back inside to see Bethany awake but barely. She sat up as soon as I came in, eyes wide.

"Change of plans," I said. "I can't take you to the shelter today. The Demons are staking us out. So you're stuck with me for another day."

She bit her lip but nodded. She didn't look surprised, just resigned. I grimaced. I hated disappointing her.

"One of the other bikers is bringing a car over," I said. "So you'll at least be able to ride more comfortably. And we'll be less conspicuous."

"When will they be here?" She asked.

"Probably in an hour or so." I ran my fingers through

my hair. "I'm sorry. This isn't what I wanted. You have to believe me."

"I do." She looked down at her hands. "I do believe you." She sounded as surprised by that revelation as I felt. She looked up at me. "I mean, you've already been so nice to me. Even when you didn't have to be nice to me. And I want to believe you."

"I'm glad, little one," I said. I sat down on the edge of the bed, making sure I was at least several feet away from her. "I want you to feel safe with me."

She bit her lip. "Can I ask you a question?"

"Of course. You can ask me anything."

"Why do you call me little one?"

7

Bethany

Something close to panic entered his gaze when I asked the question. He looked away. "Uh, I'm sorry," he said. "I didn't realize I was doing that."

"You've only done it a couple of times. I don't mind it." Somehow it felt... comfy. I didn't know how else to describe it. But it made me feel safe and protected when he called me that.

"I shouldn't be calling you that. I'll stop."

"Why not?" I asked. He seemed mad again, like last night. But this time I knew he wasn't mad at me. I just didn't understand why he would be mad at himself for this.

He took a deep breath. "Because I shouldn't be thinking about you that way."

I pulled my knees up to my chest and hugged them.

"Do you want to fuck me?" I couldn't think about what else it could be, if not that.

He flinched slightly. "No... yes. But it's more than that."

"Please tell me. I'm curious now."

He sighed. "Have you heard of DDLG before?"

I shook my head. "I don't think so."

"It stands for daddy dom, little girl. It's when one person is sweet and innocent. They dress and act like a little kid. They play with stuffies and color and sometimes even wear diapers. They're the Little. And the other one protects them and takes care of them. They're the Daddy."

I bit my lip, trying to picture it. Sure, some of the men who came into the Pleasure Room had wanted me to call them Daddy before. But it wasn't like what he was saying. There was no sense of protection or care. It was just another name while they used me. "So... you're a Daddy."

He nodded. "Yes. And to be honest, I keep thinking about you as if you were a Little. But you don't have to worry about that. I'll stop. I'll make myself stop."

I thought about the teddy bear he bought me. I had slept with it all night. I picked it up from the bed and hugged it tight to my chest. It felt comforting and sweet. Weirdly enough, there was something comforting and sweet about Ryker. He was scary, but I didn't think he wanted to hurt me. He would have hurt me by now if he was going to. "You want me to call you Daddy?"

"No," he said quickly. "I don't. I shouldn't have even told you."

"Why would you call me little one if you didn't want me to call you Daddy."

"I didn't realize I was doing it." He sounded so frustrated. "Not that there's any excuse. I should have been more careful."

"I don't mind."

He shook his head. "No. You've been through so much, Bethany. And the last thing you need is another man taking advantage of you."

"You've had plenty of chances to take advantage fo me and you haven't."

"I threatened you and kidnapped you. Yes, I did it to save you, but that doesn't matter. I made you terrified of me. I'm not a good guy. Not by a long shot."

I moved closer to him until I was only a few inches away. I took my time to look at him, really look at him.

Ryker looked exhausted, with defined dark circles until his eyes. He hadn't gotten a good night's sleep, that was for sure. And the cut on his eye wasn't deep but is was covered in crusted blood. He hadn't even bothered to clean it last night. His white shirt was wrinkled and dirty as well. Ryker looked like he had just come out of a war zone.

But he took the time to make sure I was clean and fed last night. He let me sleep on the bed last night. He had even given me his motorcycle helmet to protect me, even though it meant he was vulnerable to tree branches and gunshots. Even though I had struggled and tried to escape multiple times, he always put my comfort and well-being above his own.

"You are a good man, Ryker. You've been so good to me

and so kind. I... I want to call you Daddy. I want to be yours."

He shook his head, even as a look of longing crossed his face. "You don't mean that."

"I do." I cautiously reached out and put a hand on his shoulder. "I've never had a Daddy before. Not in any sense. But I want you to be my Daddy. Please. Please be my Daddy."

He groaned and turned to me. "How could I resist a request like that?" He wrapped his arms around me and pulled me up against him.

For once, I enjoyed being in a man's arms. With Ryker I felt safe. I felt like everything would be okay. Like he would protect me. I snuggled up against him, burying my face in his chest.

He planted a kiss on the top of my head. "I need you to know I'll take care of you and protect you even if you decide you don't want me as a Daddy anymore. Okay? I want you to be my Little only because you want it."

I nodded. "Yes, Daddy." I smiled. I believed him when he said he would protect me even if I changed my mind. I wasn't scared of Ryker anymore. Whether or not he believed it, he had proven to me he was a good man. And I wanted to belong to him. I wanted to make him feel as good as he made me.

I pulled away to reach up and cup his face with my hand. "You need to get cleaned up too, Daddy."

He chuckled. "I suppose you're right. I've got to take care of myself if I'm going to take care of you, don't I?"

I stood up and grabbed his hand, leading him to the bathroom. "Let me clean you up, Daddy."

"It's my job to take care of you, little one. Not the other way around."

I pouted. "But I want to help."

He looked conflicted for a second before smiling. "Okay, little one. You can clean me up."

He sat down on the toilet while I wet a washcloth with warm, soapy water. Gently, I dabbed it at the cut on his eye. Ryker seemed to relax a little and turned into my touch. "That feel so good, little one."

I smiled. "I'm glad, Daddy."

I cleaned the wound gently. It wasn't very deep, just like I thought. But it was good to clean it up a little. After I was done, I put the cloth down. Ryker grabbed my hand and kissed it, gently. "Thank you, little one."

I smiled in response. It felt good taking care of Ryker a little. Especially after he had taken such good care of me.

There was a knock on the door and Ryker tensed. "Stay here," he said.

He went to the door to investigate before suddenly relaxing. "It's all right," he said. "It's just Mac."

He opened the door to reveal a man just as tall and muscular as himself but Mac was wearing a dark t-shirt and a leather jacket. He grinned when he saw me. "Hello," he said. "My name is Mac. I'm one of the presidents of the Hell's Renegades." His voice had a nice Irish lilt to it.

"I'm Bethany," I said.

"Nice to meet you, Bethany." He turned to look back at Ryker. "You're lookin' pretty sorry, boyo. Good thing I brought you a change of clothes. He held up a backpack. "The car is ready to go as well. Take it to the safe house and Chase will contact you when the coast is clear."

"Thanks," Ryker said. He grabbed the bag from Mac. "I appreciate it."

Mac nodded and then left.

Ryker opened the bag and pulled out a leather jacket and t-shirt. "Thank god." He stripped off the white button down jacket and put on the t-shirt and jacket. He looked immediately more comfortable. Ryker turned to smile at me. "Let's get out of here," he said. "We can get some food and then go to the safehouse."

I smiled. "Sounds perfect, Daddy."

8

Ryker

I kept studying Bethany, looking for any signs of regret or fear. I couldn't believe she wanted to be my Little. It was way too good to be true. But she seemed genuinely happy as we got into the blue sedan Mac left for us. Once we were both settled in the car, she grabbed my hand as if it was the most natural thing in the world.

I wanted her to feel safe with me. I wanted to make her smile and laugh. And more than anything I wanted to deserve her. But I knew that wasn't possible. A brute like me would never deserve her.

We went through a drive-thru for breakfast, where I got her a breakfast sandwich, a blueberry muffin, and some fresh fruit, as well as a little carton of chocolate milk. She grinned happily as I handed her the food. "All of this is for me?" She asked, a little wonder in her voice.

"Of course, little one," I said. "You need to regain your

strength." I only had a cup of coffee and a breakfast sandwich for myself, which was more than enough.

She practically wolfed down the food, greedily. Just the sight of it made my chest tighten. She wouldn't ever go hungry again, not if I had anything to do with it.

After she finished eating, she curled up in the seat, her little teddy in the arms. Her eyes drifted shut as she dozed. I couldn't help but smile. She was so adorable and sweet. And I could tell she was getting stronger. Even just a full meal and a good night's rest had brought some color back into her cheeks.

I drove to the safehouse, an abandoned house in the middle of the woods. No other houses were around it.

From the street view, it looked like a condemned building that wasn't fit to be lived in.

The driveway was overgrown and full of weeds. Part of it was mostly shielded from street view by trees and and bushes. I checked to make sure no one else was on the road before pulling into the driveway, hiding the car in the forest.

I put my hand on Bethany's shoulder and gently shook it.

She stirred a little, sighing.

"Come on, little one. Time to wake up."

She sat up and looked around, looking a little dazed from her nap. "Where are we?" she asked.

"We're at the safe house," I said.

She looked up and her brow furrowed when she saw the decaying building. She didn't say anything but she chewed her lip nervously.

"It's okay," I said. "It's better than it looks, I promise."

She nodded. "Yes, Daddy."

After making sure the coast was clear, I got out of the car with her and led her around the building to the backyard, which was just as overgrown as the rest of the property.

In the back were doors leading down to the basement. I opened it up, revealing a dark staircase underneath. I glanced back at Bethany, who was still looking a little nervous and even tense. But she stayed still. She wasn't going to try to run. I couldn't help but smile a little. Even under weird circumstances like this, she trusted me enough to keep from running.

I went into the basement first and felt on the wall for the light switch. I switched on the light, revealing the basement which had been turned into a modern-looking studio apartment.

It was small and cozy, with a combined living room and kitchen with a couch that pulled out into a bed. It wasn't a lot of space, but it was completely secret from the Demons and we would be safe here.

I grabbed Bethany's hand and led her into the basement. Once we were inside, I shut and locked the door. "We'll be safe in here," I said. "Even if they do find us, they wouldn't be able to get in here without a battering ram."

She smiled. "Thank you, Daddy."

"Come here, little one." I held out my arms and she wrapped her arms around my waist. I smiled and hugged her back. "You're safe," I whispered. "And soon this will all be over."

"I know." She snuggled up against me. "As long at you're with me, I'm happy."

God, I hoped she was telling the truth.

I pulled apart. "Let's do something fun," I said. "What would you like to do? We could watch a movie, color, play a game, or something else if you prefer."

She looked up at me, biting her lip. "I-I think I want to watch a movie," she said slowly. "But would it be okay if we did something else first?"

"Of course, little one," I said. "Whatever you want."

"C-could I kiss you, Daddy?" She blushed as she spoke, as if she was nervous I would say no. Or nervous about the kiss in general.

I smoothed her hair out of her face. "I want nothing more than to kiss you right now," I said. "But are you sure you're ready for that, little one? I don't want to push you into something you're not ready for."

She nodded. "I'm ready," she said. "I want to kiss you. Please, Daddy."

I groaned softly. "Then close your eyes, little one."

Her eyes fluttered closed and I gently raised her chin so she was facing me. Gentle. I had to be gentle with her. That's what she needed. That's what she deserved.

I pressed my lips against hers and she reached out to grab onto the belt loops of my pants to keep her balance. Her lips were soft and warm and they yielded so willingly under my touch. I groaned softly as I kissed her some more. She felt so sweet and gentle.

I licked her bottom lip and they parted, letting me

inside. I explored her mouth with my tongue. She whimpered and sighed happily,

Just this simple kiss was enough to make my cock grow hard until all I could think about was claiming her body for myself. I wanted to strip her out of her sweatshirt and sweatpants, lie her down on the floor and take her over and over until she came all over my cock.

No. I couldn't think like that. I needed to be gentle with her. I needed to go slow.

I broke away from her, breathing hard. She looked up at me with a dazed expression. Her face was flushed but she wore a small smile.

I cupped her cheek with my hand. "Did you enjoy that, little one?" I asked.

She nodded. "That felt so good, Daddy. I think I like kissing you."

I smiled and pulled her into a hug. "I'm glad, Little one," I said. "I like kissing you too." I kissed the top of her head. "Now, let me set up everything for the movie. I think there are some stuffies and other things in the closet over there if you want to look.

She skipped over to the closet and looked inside while I got everything set up for a Disney movie. I was just about to make popcorn when she came out of the closet.

"Hey, Daddy?" she asked.

"Yes, little one?"

"Who's clothes are in there?"

"No one in particular," I said. "Most Hell's Renegade members are Daddies, so the safe house is stocked for both Daddies and Littles. That includes clothes, toys, and other activities."

"So if I wanted to wear one of the dresses in there, that would be okay?"

I nodded. "Absolutely, little one. You're my Little after all. I want you to feel comfy and wear whatever makes you happy."

She grinned. "Thank you, Daddy."

"I can't wait to see what you put on."

9

Bethany

Normally, I wouldn't have asked to change. The sweatshirt and sweatpants were comfy and cozy as it was. But in the closet was a pink princess dress with a puffy skirt and puffed sleeves. It looked a lot like the type of dress I wanted to wear when I was a kid.

I never got the chance to wear pretty dresses when I was little. They got dirty too fast and ripped too easily. We didn't have a lot, so my clothes had to last a long time.

The dress fit almost perfectly. I zipped it up and twirled around in the closet, giggling a little to myself.

Without the sweatpants, I realized how exposed I was. I didn't have any underwear at all and the skirt was short so my pussy would be on full display every time I moved. Maybe there would be some underwear in the closet?

There were a couple of packages of brand new frilly underwear. And they were pretty but I was drawn to a package of adult diapers. Ryker had said some Littles wear these.

I picked up one of the diapers. It was soft and cushy and kind of cute. I had never considered wearing one before, but I was curious to try it.

"Little one?" Ryker tapped softly on the door. "Are you okay in there?"

I jumped up to my feet. "Yes, Daddy. I'm sorry, I didn't mean to take so long."

"You don't have to apologize. I just wanted to make sure you were okay."

I opened the door to the walk-in closet and looked at Ryker on the other side. He was smiling down at me but there was a furrow in his brow, as if he was concerned about me. "You look beautiful," he said. "That's a very pretty dress."

I blushed and looked down. "Thank you, Daddy." I felt myself smile a goofy grin. I was used to compliments from men. I got them all the time in the Pleasure Room. I had never really cared about them before. But with Ryker, I did. I liked hearing him compliment. Just like I liked it when he kissed me.

Ryker noticed I had a diaper in my hands. "Do you want to put on a diaper, little one?"

I bit my lip and nodded. I was definitely curious about it.

Then a thought entered my mind. A scary but delicious thought. I held up the diaper to Ryker. "I'm not sure how to put on the diaper. Would you put it on me, Daddy?"

Lust flared up in his gaze and his smile disappeared. He swallowed. "Are you sure, little one?"

I nodded. "Please, Daddy. I want you to." I wanted him to see me. I wanted him to desire me. And I wanted him to know I trusted him.

"Then come out here, little one." His voice was husky with need.

I followed him out into the living room. He held out his hand and I gave him the diaper. "Lie down on your back," he commanded.

I was quick to obey. I got a little rush of pleasure every time I obeyed Ryker, unlike with the Demons where I obeyed out of fear.

"Spread your legs a little and lift up your hips."

As I lifted up my hips, I knew I was on full display for him. A thrill of excitement ran through me. I sneaked a peek at him to see what he thought.

A slight flush was on his face as he looked at me hungrily. I could see a muscle working in his jaw as he restrained himself from touching me. My pussy was completely bare, without any hair to speak of, thanks to the rules of the Pleasure Room. And there was no disguising that I was wet for him. That I wanted him.

I half expected him to say something or to reach out and touch me, but instead he focused on the diaper. He slid it under me and cleared his throat. "Okay, you can relax now."

I rested down on the soft cushion beneath me.

Ryker put the diaper together around me, careful not to actually touch me down there. Part of me was disappointed even though I appreciated his care. "How does that feel, little one?" he asked.

I wiggled my hips, getting used to the feeling of the diaper. "It feels good, Daddy," I said. "It feels comfy."

He smiled. "I'm glad, little one."

I sat up. Ryker was smiling but it was a little strained. It was easy to see why. His erection was tenting in his pants. "Did you enjoy putting the diaper on me, Daddy?"

"Yes, little one," he growled.

I put my hand on his knee. "I could make you enjoy something else as well."

He smiled softly as he grabbed my hand. But instead of moving it to his cock, he lifted it up and kissed it. "I know you could, but not right now."

I pouted. "But I want to make you feel good."

"You know what would really make me feel good? Watching a movie with my little one." He smiled as he stood up and held out his hand to help me to my feet. He reached out to brush some hair out of my eyes. "You're perfect, little one," he said. "I want you to know that you'll always please me, no matter what. And you never, ever have to do anything sexual with me to make me happy."

I frowned. "But you're going to want it eventually, right?"

"Not if you don't. Not if you're not ready." He kissed my forehead. "Taking care of you as your Daddy is already more than I could have asked for. It's more than I deserve. I'll never expect anything more."

He pulled me into a hug and I couldn't help but smile.

His arms felt so good around me. For the first time in my life, I felt completely safe and happy.

I snuggled up against him as we watched a Disney movie. I clutched the teddy bear to me as we watched. He had made popcorn as well. It wasn't long before we started a game of him tossing popcorn and me trying to catch it in my mouth. We stopped paying attention to the movie, too focused on laughing at me trying to catch the popcorn.

He threw the last piece of popcorn up high and I moved to catch it. I launched myself into the air and caught it before landing in his lap, giggling.

Ryker grinned down at me. "Okay, little one, that's enough popcorn for now." He put the empty bowl off to the side.

I snuggled up in his lap, leaning my head against his shoulder. "I'm sleepy, Daddy."

"I bet. You've had a long couple of days."

I sighed. "But I've had more sleep these past two days than I've had in... forever."

"Yes, but you've been through hell. It's going to take you awhile to recover." He set me down on the couch and stood up. "How about I make up the bed for you and you can take a nap?"

"Only if you stay with me."

Heat flared in his gaze. "If that's what you want, little one."

I helped him pull the bed out of the couch and get it all set up. Then we snuggled down into the blankets. I put my arm around his waist and tangled my legs with his. He played with my hair.

As we lied there, I kept looking at his tattoos. He had a lot of them, which were visible when he was only in a t-shirt. I reached out to trace a scorpion on his forearm. "This is cool," I said.

He smiled. "You like it?"

I nodded. "Tattoos are pretty. This one it nice." My fingers traveled up his arm to one even higher. It was a serpent wrapped around a rose. "This one is really pretty. It's like the snake is protecting the flower."

"You think so?"

"You don't?"

"It could be destroying it. Suffocating it."

I shook my head. "No. I don't think so. See how it's snarling at us? It's like it's warning us that it's his flower and nobody had better hurt it." I looked up at him. "Right?"

He smiled softly. "I like your interpretation of it much better, little one."

I pushed the hem of his t-shirt up to reveal his stomach. He sucked in his breath but he didn't move. I traced more tattoos on his waist. There were knives and skulls, but also dragonflies and flowers. They were so pretty and I got lost in tracing the designs with my fingers. I was tracing the Hell's Renegade logo when he gasped slightly. He cleared his throat. "I should do a quick patrol outside," he said. "And make sure no one's found us."

"I thought you said we were safe here," I said. "And

wouldn't you walking around outside draw more attention."

He smiled slightly. "You're very smart, little one. Definitely no fooling you. It was silly of me to try." He smoothed back my hair. The gesture was simple but it made me feel warm inside. "Honestly, you touching me like this, admiring my tattoos... it's made me want you. I've been trying to keep my hands off you, to treat you like you deserve, but being this close to you while you look this adorable... it's taking all of my control to keep from taking you."

"What if I want you to take me?"

He shook his head slowly. "How could you possibly want that, little one? After what you've been through? After what I did to you?" He clenched his jaw.

"You saved me, Daddy. Sure, you were a little rough, but you were just trying to get me to safety."

"I made you afraid of me."

"And that got me out of there alive. When will you stop beating yourself up over that?"

"Never. I should have found another way."

I huffed. "Well, I don't blame you for it." I got on top of him so I was straddling him. "And I want you, Daddy. I want all of you."

"You have me," he growled. "You'll always have me."

I smiled and leaned down to kiss him. He groaned softly as his arms wrapped around my waist. His hand went to my hair as our lips melded together. His tongue entered my mouth, exploring it. "Please take me, Daddy," I whispered against his lips.

He groaned and flipped me over on my back. "You're so fucking beautiful, little one," he said as he trailed kisses down my neck. "I can't believe you're mine." His hand went up my thigh to my diaper-covered pussy. Slowly, he pulled down the diaper to reveal my pussy underneath. As he kissed my neck, his finger touched my clit, making me gasp and whimper.

His tongue entered my mouth as he pushed a finger inside me. I moaned and started moving my hips, trying to take his finger deeper and deeper inside me.

"You're so wet, little one," he said. "You're so wet for Daddy, aren't you?" His thumb started teasing my clit.

"Yes, Daddy," I whimpered.

"I want you to come for Daddy," he whispered in my ear. "Can you do that for me, little one?"

I could already feel the pleasure building inside me as he kissed the crook of my neck while he played with my clit and thrust a finger in and out of me. I couldn't reply to him. I couldn't even talk. I was too lost in the pleasure.

Soon I went over the edge and came all over his hand with a burst of pleasure that left me shaking.

"Good girl," he murmured. "You're such a good girl for Daddy."

"I want more," I whimpered. "I want your cock. Please, Daddy, I want your cock."

He groaned. "You can have it, little one." He unbuttoned his pants and pulled out his thick, hard cock. He positioned it at my entrance before pausing. "Are you absolutely sure?" he asked.

"Yes, Daddy," I said. "Please."

He pushed his cock into me slowly. Ryker let out a shuddering groan as he went slow, achingly slow. "Fuck, you're beautiful," he whispered.

I moved my hips, wanting him in deeper. "Go faster, Daddy. Please. You won't hurt me."

He chuckled. "If you say so, little one." He grabbed my hips with both hands and started thrusting into me, faster and faster. I moaned and wrapped my arms around his neck, losing myself in the pleasure as he claimed my body. I could feel another orgasm building inside me. "I-I'm going to come, Daddy."

"Then come," he growled. "Come all over my cock." He gripped my hips tighter and I came. The orgasm turned me into a shuddering, gasping mess as my pussy pulsated around him. The force of it was enough to send him over the edge. He let out a shaky gasp as he came, his hot seed filling me up.

For a moment, there wasn't anything except the sounds of us breathing as we recovered from our orgasms. Then he rolled off me and gathered me up into his arms. "Are you okay, little one?" he asked. "How to you feel?"

I smiled as I snuggled up against him. "I feel wonderful, Daddy," I said. "I feel absolutely perfect."

He smiled, looking relieved. "I'm glad."

He held me for awhile. I was just starting to drift off to sleep when his phone buzzed. I lifted up my head as he picked it up. "Is everything okay?" Nerves fluttered in my stomach. What if the Demons had found us? Or they had overtaken the rest of the Hell's Renegades? What then?

But Ryker just snorted as he looked at his phone. "Perfect timing," he said. "Chase just texted me. They managed to scare the Demons back into their own territory for the time being. We're free."

"So what happens now?" I asked.

He started to play with my hair which made me smile. "That depends. You could stay with me. Or if you're not ready for that, I could set you up with an apartment somewhere. Close enough so I could see you. But you would have your own space and as much independence as you want."

"I want to stay with you," I said immediately. "Please, Daddy."

He smiled at me. "Of course, little one. Of course you can stay with me." He kissed my forehead. "I love you," he whispered.

"I love you too, Daddy." I smiled. How could I have gotten so lucky to get a Daddy like Ryker? I closed my eyes and buried my face in his chest. I waas with my Daddy. Forever.

WILD BIKER DADDY

1

Ella

My little sister and her boyfriend were fighting again. That wasn't anything new. They were always fighting. I looked at my phone. It was close to midnight and I needed to be at work in the morning.

I grimaced and got out of my twin-sized bed. My sister and I lived in a crappy one-bedroom apartment and the walls weren't exactly soundproof. So I could hear all the screaming from the living room easily and there was no way I would be able to fall asleep with it.

I went into the living room. "Hey!" I shouted.

Neither of them heard me. Lindsey was continuing to scream at her boyfriend, who was just known at Foghorn. "Lindsey!" I shouted.

Finally, they looked at me. Foghorn's expression immediately went from one of rage to polite cordiality. I hated how quickly he seemed to shift moods. It was disconcerting and made me think he was being deceptive.

Of course, being deceptive was probably his specialty, working for sketchy organization like the Demon biker gang.

"You guys need to stop," I said, looking at both of them. "It's almost midnight and I'm working in the morning. And the neighbors are going to complain." I didn't know what we would do if we got a noise complaint and got kicked out. We could barely afford this place as it was and there was no way we would find a place as cheap as this.

"I'm sorry," Lindsey said. She took a deep breath to try and calm down. "We'll try to keep it down."

"No. Foghorn, you need to leave for the night."

"What?" His face twisted into surprise and then into anger. "No, we're not done here. Stay out of it, Ella."

I clenched my hands into fists. I hated confrontation. Every part of me wanted to run and hide. But I took a deep breath and steeled myself. "Get out or I'm calling the police."

He sneered. "Fine. But this isn't over, Lindsey." He left, slamming the door on his way out. Lindsey and I both flinched from the sound.

"You didn't have to be so rude to him," Lindsey said.

I sighed and rubbed my forehead. "I can't talk about this with you, Lindsey. I have to get some sleep."

"Oh come on, you have the energy to kick my boyfriend out but not talk to me?"

"You know perfectly well why I had to kick him out." I

looked pointedly down at her exposed wrist, covered in a bruise. Lindsey said it was an accident and that he had grabbed her too quickly. He hadn't meant to be rough with her. But I found that hard to believe.

She pulled her sleeve over her wrist and glared at me. "Don't pretend you did that for me. You did that just to get your beauty sleep."

"Lindsey, I haven't slept in 48 hours because I was up all night last night working overtime logging inventory at work so we could buy groceries. Sue me for wanting to get in a few hours of sleep before getting up to work again."

"You act like you're the only one here who works," she said. "I'm also pulling double shifts. I'm also doing gig work to pay the bills. We're all exhausted."

I took a deep breath. This fight wasn't going anywhere. "I know," I said. "I know we both work a lot and I'm sorry. We can continue this conversation in the morning. Goodnight."

I went back to the bedroom and got into bed. I sighed and closed my eyes. I was so tired. But not just from lack of sleep. I was tired of always feeling like the one in charge. Even when we were kids, I was always expected to be a role model and set an example for Lindsey. If Lindsey misbehaved, I also got in trouble because I never taught her any better. And now we were both adults but I still felt like I had to set a good example. And I felt like I was failing at it now.

I asleep before Lindsey entered the room to sleep on her own twin-sized bed, only to be woken up by my alarm, way too early.

I groaned and sat up, trying to blink the sleep out of my eyes. I felt like I was in a daze. I got up and dragged myself out to the kitchen. To my surprise, there was already coffee made. Had Lindsey woken up before me? Did she even go asleep last night?

Lindsey and I shared a room, but I was so tired, I didn't even notice if she was in the room or not.

There was a note by the coffee maker. "Ella– I'm sorry we fought last night. I'm going to try to make some more money today. Maybe once we have a little in savings, we can both relax a little more. Love, Lindsey."

I winced. I didn't mean to make Lindsey feel bad. I knew she worked hard. She worked at a retail store in Middleton, which was one town over. Even though we both worked minimum wage, she didn't get commission bonuses like I did. She tried to make up for it by doing some gig work, but there was only so much work to go around.

I hoped she didn't try to push herself too hard. She needed to rest too. More than anything, she needed to break up with her useless boyfriend, but there was no convincing her of that.

I poured some coffee into a travel mug and drove to the Newbury Mall, where I worked.

It was a sad place that looked more abandoned than not, but there were still a couple of restaurants open in the food court and a couple of retail stores. There was also an Irish pub that had just opened up called the Celtic Knot. I steered clear of that place. It was a biker hangout and after meeting Foghorn, I wanted nothing to do with bikers.

I worked at a clothing store chain that was the sole sign of life in one section of the mall. It didn't open for another hour, but my manager, Terry, was already there getting things set up. "You're late," he said.

I looked at my watch. I was actually two minutes early. But Terry considered five minutes early on time and everything else was late.

"Your sales are down this week," he continued as he set up the cash register.

"No one has been coming in," I argued. "I've made a sale on most customers who come in."

He glared at me. "Did I ask for your excuses? No. The only competitive edge we have over online retail is customer service. Clearly, you're not delivering."

I stayed silent while Terry lectured me. It wasn't worth arguing. He wouldn't listen anyway.

When the store opened, Terry disappeared into his office, leaving me to run the store by myself. I went to the cash register while watching the entrance, wondering if anyone would even enter the store today.

To my surprise, two people entered almost at the same time. My heart sank when I saw who it was. One of them was my landlord. The other was a biker.

2

Crowe

It was my first time being anywhere in the Newbury mall other than The Celtic Knot. The rest of the mall was so depressing, I didn't spend much time in it at all. But I needed to buy something for my cousin and I figured a salesperson could help me better than an internet search.

The store had just opened and it looked like there was only one person working, a petite woman at the register. I could tell from a glance that she was tired and probably not in the best of moods, even though she gave me a strained smile when I entered. I smiled back and started to approach her but another man entered at the same time and he beat me to her. "Ella," he said. "Glad I was able to catch you."

"Hello, Charles," she said. She didn't sound happy to see him.

I decided to look at a nearby jewelry case to see if

anything caught my eye while I waited for her to be available.

"There was a noise complaint last night," Charles was saying. "I gave you a deal when I gave you that apartment because I thought you were cute, but I didn't know you would be so much trouble."

"I'm sorry," Ella said. "It won't happen again."

He gave an exaggerated sigh. I was liking this guy less by the minute. "It's the third time this month, Ella. I might have to evict you. I would hate to see a pretty thing like you end up in a shelter though."

"What do you want?" she hissed. "What do you want from me?" Her voice broke. She was holding back tears. I forced myself to keep my gaze on the jewelery case. If I even looked at them I would end up beating his face in for harassing her like this.

"I could be persuaded to look the other way," he said. "If you make it worth my while."

"Are you blackmailing me?"

"Frankly, yes," he said. "You could give me cash. Or you could show up on my doorstep and give me something of a more personal nature."

My hands clenched into fists.

She took a shuddering breath. "I get paid tomorrow afternoon. I'll get you the money then."

"I want it tonight. Or you'll wake up to an eviction notice on your door tomorrow morning."

That was it. I couldn't keep standing by while this happened. I went over to both of them. "Good morning," I said. "I'm short on time and patience. How about I pay whatever blackmail you want and you go away right now?" I glared at Charles.

He paled as he looked up at me. I was easily three inches taller than him and outweighed him with at least twenty pounds of solid muscle. And I wouldn't hesitate to hurt him if he so much as looked at the saleswoman again. "I wasn't blackmailing anyone," he said. "And you shouldn't be eavesdropping."

"Let's get one thing clear: the only reason I'm being this civil is because there's a lady present. So how much will it take to make you go away?"

He swallowed. "Three hundred."

I took out my wallet and pulled out three hundred dollars and threw it at his feet. "If I find out you're harassing her or anyone else, I'm going to make your life very unpleasant, *Charles*."

He scooped it up and glared at me as if he was trying to look intimidating while backing away from me and all but running out of the exit.

I turned to see Ella scowling. "You shouldn't have done that," she said, crossing her arms. "I will pay you back. If you give me your name and number, I'll get you the money when my paycheck comes."

"I don't want money, or anything else," I said. "But my name is Crowe."

She rolled her eyes. "Of course it is."

I raised an eyebrow. Bikers didn't have the best reputation in Newbury. The town had been ripped apart by the Demon biker gang. Even though me and the rest of the Hell's Renegades had moved into town and beaten them away for the most part, the scars ran deep. But this was probably the most openly hostile someone had acted towards me so far. "I paid him off because I'm short on time. All I need is your expertise as a salesperson." I had time to spare. But the last thing I wanted was her thinking I paid him off because I wanted to exploit her myself."

She forced a smile to her face, but it looked strained. "What are you looking for?"

"I'm looking for a birthday present for my cousin. I'm not sure what to get her."

"Is she a biker too?"

"No, that would make it easy. She likes swimming, hiking, and kickboxing. Overall, she's pretty athletic, I guess."

Ella paused, seeming to think. "Well, we have some pretty nice athletic pants in all sorts of colors. Let me show you."

She led me to the back of the store, stifling a yawn on the way there. When was the last time she had a good night's sleep? Or a decent meal? I couldn't help but notice how her uniform hung off her body as if it was two sizes too big. In fact, she looked like a stiff breeze could knock her over.

"What do you think of these?" She turned around and took a step back, flinching. Even though I was a foot away from her, it was closer than she had been expecting. She tried to hide her fear behind a smile again, but she wasn't quite successful.

"I'm not with the Demons, you know," I said. "You don't have to be afraid of me."

She looked away. "Look, I don't know the difference between Demons or any other biker. I'm sorry I flinched, but don't take it personally. I'm just a jumpy person."

I didn't believe that. She hadn't flinched around her landlord. She had been upset and desperate. But not scared. I scared her. "I'm part of the Hells Renegades. We own the Celtic Knot, which is on the other side of the mall. We try to help people, not hurt them."

"I believe you," she said. Her tone said the opposite. "A-anyway, what do you think of these pants?"

I ended up getting a pair of blue pants with pink roses on them. On our way to the register, we passed the winter clothes section and a thought occurred to me. "Hey, do you work on commission?"

She gave me a wary look. "I do. Why?"

I grabbed several pairs of gloves, hats, and scarves, as many as I can carry. "Then I'll be getting these as well."

She looked bewildered and then angry. "I'm already in your debt, I don't see why you have to make it worse."

"You're not in my debt at all," I said as I set the pile of winter clothes on the counter. "You were really helpful. I want to make sure you benefit." Hopefully the commission would be enough for her to buy some decent food.

"So you're buying a bunch of stuff you don't have any use for?"

"I'm sure the homeless shelter will have use for them. It's been pretty cold lately."

She looked down as she scanned the items. "I guess you're not the worst biker I've met," she said.

I smirked. "High praise."

She finished ringing me up and I paid for the items in cash. When she was finished, she handed me my receipt. "I hope you have a great day."

"I will. I hope you do too." I hesitated for a second before grabbing a pen and scribbling my number on the back of my receipt. "This isn't me trying to get a date or anything, but here's my number. I just want you to know you can call me if your landlord tries to blackmail you again. I'll take care of it. No questions asked and no strings attached." I shrugged. "Or you can throw it away. It's up to you."

She frowned. "But you don't even know me. For all you know, I'll give out your number to a bunch of scam websites."

I grinned. "Then I'll look forward to a bunch of shady text messages about my car's extended warranty. Like I said, it's up to you. Have a good day, Ella."

I left without waiting for a reply. I knew she would probably just throw away my number. But I wanted to give her the option anyway. I didn't like the thought of someone getting hurt. Especially when I could stop it.

3

Ella

Despite the excitement from the morning, the rest of the day went by uneventfully. There were only a couple of small sales before my shift ended. Nothing like the huge purchase Crowe had made. With the commission from that sale, I would be able to stash a little money into savings. At least until the next time I got a flat tire or broke my cell phone, or some other unforeseen accident.

I should have thrown his number away, but something made me pocket it. I didn't trust Crowe. He was still a biker after all, even if he wasn't with the Demons. But I appreciated him getting me out of that situation with Charles. Just the thought of sleeping with Charles to keep from being evicted made me want to hurl.

As I left the mall, I was careful to avoid going past the Celtic Knot. I didn't want to run into Crowe again.

I drove home. The apartment was quiet and empty. "Lindsey?" I called. No response.

I checked my phone. No message from her. She was supposed to be here by now.

I realized I had one new voicemail from an unknown number. It was probably a robocall, but I decided to listen anyway. As soon as I hit play, Lindsey's panicked voice seemed to blare into the room. "Ella, you have to pick up," she said. "I-I made a mistake. Foghorn told me he had a job for me, but he lied. I'm a prisoner here and they're making me do... things. Call the police. Call somebody. I–"

Somebody shouted and I couldn't make it out, but it sounded like swears. Then the line went dead.

I felt nauseous. Even though my stomach was empty, I had to swallow down the urge to throw up. Lindsey was in serious danger. I knew Foghorn was bad. And now he... I couldn't even think it. If I did, I would start panicking. And I couldn't panic. Lindsey needed me right now.

I tried to take a deep breath and I called the police. I told them my story over the phone. The officer on the other end sounded skeptical. "Are you sure this wasn't just a prank?" he said. "You said you and your sister were fighting. Maybe she was trying to get back at you."

"This wasn't a prank. I know her. She wouldn't do that. Can you just send someone down here to listen to the voicemail? My sister is in danger."

The officer sighed. "Look, it wouldn't do you much good. If she's missing for 48 hours, you can file a report, but until then, we can't do anything. She was probably pranking you, or freaking out for no reason. Chances are, she'll come back tonight, and it'll be all forgotten."

"My sister isn't a liar!" I shouted. "She wouldn't pretend she was in trouble as a prank! Something happened to her."

"Look, lady, you can file a report in 48 hours. Until then, there's nothing I can do."

I couldn't find the words to respond. My entire throat felt like it was closing up. I hung up the phone. Anger and grief were battling inside of me and I didn't know what to do. I felt so lost. And the police weren't going to help me.

Before I could think better of it, I fished out the crumpled receipt that had Crowe's number on it. Maybe he wasn't that bad. He said he wasn't a Demon. And he saved me from Charlie. He also bought a lot of things to donate to the homeless shelter for... reasons. I had meant it when I said he wasn't the worst Demon I had met.

But this was a huge favor. He would want something in return. But it didn't matter as long as I got Lindsey back and she was safe.

I dialed Crowe's number. He answered almost immediately. "Hello?"

"It's Ella," I said. Somehow my voice was calm. Resigned. "I need your help."

4

Crowe

After leaving the clothing store, I stopped by the Celtic Knot. It was empty except for Blaine, wiping down the bar. The big Irish man raised an eyebrow as I dumped my shopping bags on one of the tables. "I thought you were going to buy your cousin a birthday present. Not even I like my cousin that much."

I smirked. He and his cousin Mac, who was one of the presidents for the Hell's Renegades, were pretty close, more like brothers. But he was right. Four shopping bags' worth of presents would be excessive. "Most of these are donations for the homeless shelter. It's getting cold. And I had some extra cash on me after beating your ass in poker last week."

Blaine raised his eyebrows. "You spent all of your winnings on stuff to donate? Are you aiming for sainthood, boyo?"

I shrugged and sat down at the bar. "It's more than that. The saleswoman who helped me works on commission. Looked like she could use a break."

Blaine grinned. "Now it makes sense."

"It's not like that."

"Of course not. It's never like that." His Irish accent got thicker with the sarcasm.

I rolled my eyes. "Can I get something to eat or are you going to keep fucking with me?"

"I'm a multitasker by nature. But I'll get you some grub. One Scotch egg, comin' up. You want a coffee with that? Maybe with a little Irish cream?"

"No Irish cream," I said. "I'm not staying long. After breakfast, I'm going to drop off the donations and get going. I've got some work to do."

I lived out of town, in a house in the middle of the woods. Even though I enjoyed being part of the Hell's Renegades, I preferred being surrounded by trees. It allowed me peace and solitude after the horrors from fighting back the Demons every week. I volunteered as a wildlands firefighter, but I made my living building custom-made motorcycles from scrap parts. And I had a couple of orders to fill.

Blaine set a cup of hot coffee in front of me. After a few minutes, he came back with a Scotch egg and a couple of slices of toast. "So this saleswoman. Did you get her number?"

"No. Like I said, it wasn't like that." I took a sip of my coffee. "But I gave her mine. In case she needed help."

He raised an eyebrow. "Wow. She must have been in some rough shape."

"I came in at the right time. Her landlord came in and tried to blackmail her for a date. I stepped in. Made her angry and probably scared her half to death."

"She was scared?" He raised his eyebrows. Blaine hated people who tried to scare others into submission. He met his old lady, Hannah, by saving her from her abusive uncle. Blaine probably wouldn't have been as civil as me with the landlord. He would have dragged him out of the store and left him bleeding on the pavement.

"She was scared of me. Not of the landlord. I don't think she likes bikers much. And she probably threw out my number as soon as I left, but I wanted to give her the option anyway." I hoped she kept my number. I would love an excuse to beat that bastard into a bloody mess.

After breakfast, I left the Celtic Knot. I got on my motorcycle and biked to the homeless shelter. I dropped off most of my bags into the donation bin, aside from the present for my cousin. I smiled. I least some people would be a bit warmer this winter. Newbury was in rough shape after the Demons decimated the town and the community. Me and the rest of the Hell's Renegades were trying to make it better, but it was slow going. But even small things like clothing donations would help.

I got back on my motorcycle and prepared to drive home when my phone rang. It was an unknown number. But I decided to answer it anyway. "Hello?"

"It's Ella. I need your help."

She sounded calm. But something was wrong. She

wouldn't be calling me if she thought there was any other option. "Where are you?" I asked.

She gave me her address and I gunned it down the street.

In Newbury, there wasn't really a good part of town. All of it was pretty sleazy. But Ella's street was worse than most. I rocked up to a dilapidated apartment building that was covered in graffiti. The stench of cigarette smoke and old booze hung in the air, even though it was only early afternoon. The stench only got worse when I entered the building. How anyone could live here was beyond me.

I went up to Ella's apartment door and knocked. "Ella? It's Crowe."

"Come in," she said. "It's unlocked." Her voice sounded hoarse. As if she had been crying.

I opened the door and found her sitting on the kitchen floor. Tears were running down her face and her shoulders were shaking. She barely looked up when I came in. "My sister. She's..." her face crumpled up.

"Hang on," I said. I opened a cupboard and found a glass. I filled it with water and handed it to her. "Drink," I commanded. "All of it. Then you can tell me."

She started to sip the water and then started to drink faster. By the time she was finished, she looked calmer instead of being on the verge of tears.

I knelt down next to her on the floor. "What happened?" I asked. "Was it your landlord?"

She shook her head. "No. It's my sister." She looked up at me suddenly. "You hate the Demons, right? Promise me you hate the Demons."

"I hate them," I said. I didn't even hesitate. "They're absolute scum. What did they do?"

"My sister Lindsey is dating one of them." She took a shaky breath. "We fought yesterday about money." Her voice broke but she cleared her throat. "And her boyfriend said he had a job for her. One that would earn a lot of money."

A heavy stone entered my stomach. I had a feeling I knew where her sister was and it wasn't pretty.

Ella pressed something on her phone and a woman's panicked voice played on speaker. I listened to the whole message, including the end where someone had cut her off. Ella had started trembling again as the message played. "I'll do anything," she said. "But please help me find her. Help me keep her safe."

"I will. I'll get her back. I promise. But first you need to pack a bag. You can't stay here tonight."

"What? Why?" Her eyes were wide.

"The Demons know where you live and what car you drive, right? Foghorn's been here before. You'll be next. They'll come for you. I'm going to get you out of here."

She nodded shakily and got to her feet. "I'll be quick," she said. "I'll just pack a few things."

I waited in the kitchen as she went to her bedroom to pack. I paced around the tiny kitchen, feeling on edge. She had been in this apartment alone with the door unlocked. If Foghorn had come back to collect her, she would have been a sitting duck.

I heard the roar of a motorcycle outside and looked to see a strange figure outside. He was glaring up at the building and he pulled something out of his pocket. He threw it towards the window.

I turned just in time before glass exploded from the window shattering. Something started smoking and my eyes teared up. The person must have thrown a smoke bomb inside. I tried to find it, but it was impossible to see anything. I covered my mouth with my shirt as I started to make my way to Ella's room. At least my firefighter training could help me out now. We would be able to get out of here without too much of a problem.

Something else clattered to the floor. Something with a loud beeping. "Shit," I muttered. "Ella! Where are you? Talk to me!"

"Crowe? What's happening. Oh god–" She started coughing.

I followed the sound of her voice and reached out to grab her arm. I pulled her to the door just as the beeping got louder and faster.

We made it out of the apartment. I pushed her to the ground and fell on top of her, shielding her body with my own, just as a loud explosion happened behind us.

My ears rang from the crash. There was a pounding in the back of my head. Water poured down over us from the sprinklers in the ceiling. I took deep breaths, forcing myself to focus. I needed to get Ella out of here.

Luckily, she didn't look hurt, just shaken up. I picked myself up before grabbing her hands and pulling her up. "We need to get out of here," I said.

She was staring at the charred ruins that used to be her apartment. "My home," she whispered.

I wanted to give her time to recover from the shock. But I couldn't. The Demons might come back to make sure the deed was done.

I pulled her down the hall and to the entrance of the building. We reached my bike in seconds. "Get on behind me and grab my waist. Hold on tight."

As soon as her arms wrapped around my waist, I sped out of there and headed straight for the Celtic Knot.

We rocked up to the mall parking lot and I parked. I glanced at her as we entered the mall. She looked a little daze. I couldn't imagine what she was feeling right now. First her sister goes missing and then her apartment blew up. Now she was at the mercy of a man she barely knew and definitely didn't trust. I only hoped I could help her as much as I wanted to.

5

Ella

Crowe led me into the Celtic Knot. It was now mid-afternoon and the place was packed by bikers. They all seemed to stop to stare at us as we came in. I kept my eyes trained to the ground, too scared to make eye contact.

I would do anything to save Lindsey, but being in this bar with all of these bikers scared the shit out of me.

Crowe put his arm around my shoulders and steered me through the bar to the back. He rapped his knuckles on the door. "Chase! Open up."

The door swung open and a hulking man was on the other side. He looked from Crowe to me. His eyes lingered on me, looking me up and down. I took a step back from him on instinct.

"It's okay," Crowe said. "Chase is the club president. He can help."

Chase stepped aside to let us inside his office. Across

from his desk was a small couch. Crowe and I both sat down. Chase leaned against the edge of his desk, his arms crossed. "What happened?"

Crowe told him everything, from my sister going missing to my apartment blowing up. I felt grateful he was telling it. I felt completely spent. I didn't want to talk about it anymore. I didn't want to be in charge anymore. Luckily, Crowe was able to take the lead.

After Chase had heard the story and listened to the voicemail, he was thoughtful. "She's probably in Middleton," he said. "That's where their base of operations is right now. But after our last attack, they've heightened their security." He rubbed the back of his neck. "We'll have to be smart about this. But we'll get her out."

"The police said they couldn't do anything," I said.

Chase snorted. "Of course they said that. They're in the Demon's pocket. They won't do anything. But we'll get your sister out. I promise."

"Can you grab her something hot to drink?" Crowe asked. "And maybe something to eat as well."

"I don't need food. I need my sister." I was so anxious and exhausted, I didn't think I would be able to stomach anything even if I tried.

"We'll get you your sister," Crowe said. "But you also need to eat and drink something."

Chase left to get me something to eat and drink while I was alone with Crowe. He started pacing around the room, thinking. I hoped he was trying to figure out a plan to get Lindsey back. He and the Hell's Renegades were my best chance because the police weren't willing to help.

I knew I would have to pay up later. And Crowe knew I didn't have money. So there was really only one thing I could give him.

I studied him as he moved. At least he was better looking than Charles. My landlord made my skin crawl. Crowe was terrifying. He was at least a foot taller than me and I could tell he was built under the leather jacket. But he moved with grace despite being so big. His black hair fell down to his shoulders, but it was currently tied back into a ponytail. He had a neatly trimmed dark beard that made the bottom half of his face look like it was covered in a shadow. My guess was he was about ten years older than me.

So far he had been nice to me. He had even protected me when the bomb went off. Maybe he would be gentle with me. Maybe it wouldn't hurt too bad.

Who was I kidding? I was a virgin. And he was a scary biker. He might be nice *now,* but that would all change when it was time for me to pay up.

Chase came back in with a tray of food. It included some hot tea and and soup. "Here you go," he said. "This will warm you up."

"Thank you," I said. I bit my lip. "Um, I don't have any money on me." My purse was probably blown to bits along with the rest of my apartment.

"It's on the house," he said. "Special rate for people who get blown up by the Demons."

"Why would they try to blow you up?" Crowe asked. "It was the middle of the day. That feels careless even for them."

"Foghorn hated me," I said. "I tried to get Lindsey to break up with him and he knew that. He probably wanted me out of the way." I swallowed. I had known he was bad news, but I didn't think he would actually try to kill me.

"Then he might try again," said Chase. "Here's what's going to happen. Diesel, Blaine, and I are going to go out in the middle of the night and get Lindsey back. But in the meantime, Crowe is going to take you back to his place. His house is basically a safehouse and he can protect you while we send a message to the Demons. By the time we're done, they won't mess with you or your sister again."

I bit my lip. I hadn't expected to be going back to Crowe's place so soon. But it was okay. As long as Lindsey got away from the Demons, it would be okay. "Thank you," I said.

Chase smirked. "Trust me, any chance to piss of the Demons is worth it. I'll leave you two alone. Wait until night to leave. And there's a change of clothes for Ella in the closet."

"Is that really necessary?" Crowe asked. He was frowning.

Chase nodded. "The night will protect you a little, but a disguise will help. If the Demons are watching us, then they'll see you two leave and they will follow."

Crowe sighed and rubbed the back of his head. "Fine."

I didn't understand what they were saying. What disguise? And why would there be clothes for me if Chase hadn't known I was coming?

Chase left me and Crowe alone and I looked at him, wanting answers. He didn't look happy.

"I'm sorry about this," he said.

"I don't understand what's happening."

"The Demons might be watching us. If they want to kill you, then they'll follow us when we leave. That's why we have to be careful. If we leave at night, they won't see our faces as well. And you can hide in plain sight as my old lady."

I frowned. "That's what Foghorn had called Lindsey."

He clenched his jaw but nodded. "Yes. It means significant other."

I took a deep breath. "Okay," I said. "So this means I would be dressed like a biker, right? Leather jacket? Combat boots?" What else did bikers wear?

Crowe shook his head slowly. "No. You'll be dressed as my Little."

6

Crowe

How was I supposed to explain this to Ella? She barely trusted me. To her, I was no better than the man who stole her sister. And now I was asking her to pretend to be my Little?

But Chase was right. This was the safest way to get her out of here.

Ella sipped her tea while I tried to find the words to explain to her. She had barely touched her soup. If she didn't have an appetite now, she definitely wouldn't after I tried to explain myself. "The Hell's Renegades have a certain type when it comes to old ladies," I said. "Have you heard of DDLG before?"

Her brow furrowed and she shook her head. "I-is that some sort of sex thing?" Her eyes went wide. She looked absolutely terrified.

"No," I said quickly. "I mean, not always. It means

Daddy Dom, Little Girl. The Daddy takes care of their Little. Spoils them. Loves them. And the Little is free to act like a little kid and express themselves however they want. They color, play with stuffies, read books, and follow rules set out by the Daddy. And they tend to wear little kid clothes. Onesies, puffy dresses, and things like that."

Ella stared at me, processing this. "So you want me to call you Daddy?"

Part of me did. Something about Ella brought out my Daddy instincts. She was so vulnerable and adorable. I wanted to be her Daddy. But she was scared of me. I couldn't even let myself entertain that thought. "You don't have to," I said. "I think you wearing the clothes will be enough to take off suspicion. But I wanted to explain it anyway."

She bit her lip. "You said Littles have to follow rules. What if they break a rule?"

I was surprised she was so curious about it. Maybe she was trying to distract herself from thinking about her sister or the Demons. "Then the Daddy punishes them," I said. "The rules are laid out beforehand and if they are broken, then there's punishment. Sometimes it's a time out, sometimes it's a spanking. Nothing that actually hurts the Little. Littles aren't supposed to be afraid of their Daddies. They're supposed to feel safe with them."

She nodded. "That makes sense."

I rubbed the back of my neck, feeling a little awkward. The more I talked about this with her, the easier it was to see her as my Little. And I couldn't think of her like that. She made it very clear she didn't want a biker. After her sister was safe, I would have to be prepared to never see her again. "You should eat some soup," I said. "It's a long drive to my place and you'll need your strength."

She looked down. "I'm not that hungry."

"Have you had anything to eat today?"

She hesitated for a second before shaking her head. "I had ramen noodles last night for dinner."

Fuck. It was a miracle she hadn't passed out from hunger today. "I need you to eat, then," I said. "Can you eat ten bites of soup for me?"

She nodded and picked up the bowl. "Yes," she said, her voice a little higher pitched. She sounded exactly like a Little. The sound of it made my blood heat up.

"Good girl." The praise escaped me before I could think better of it.

She blushed from my words and she looked down at her food without replying. I could have kicked myself. She was already uncomfortable around me and I was just making it worse.

Ella ended up eating all of the soup. When she was finished, she looked a little more relaxed. "Thank you," she said. "After eating the first bite, I got hungry."

I smiled. "Good. You needed it."

There was a small closet behind Chase's desk. I opened it and found a lot of extra clothes, stuffies, and coloring books inside. They all belonged to his old lady, Melody, but plenty of the other old ladies borrowed them when they came to the Celtic Knot.

I picked out a dark green dress and black ballet flats. They looked like they were roughly Ella's size. I laid them out on the desk. I also pulled out an adult diaper and put it on the table as well. I told myself if would help sell the bit. After all, you would have to be pretty committed to a disguise as a Little if you were willing to wear an adult diaper. But if I was being honest, I wanted her to wear it. I wanted to know she was in a cute little diaper. "I'll give you some privacy to change. Just tap on the door when you're done."

"Thank you," she said. "I appreciate it."

I stepped outside and closed the door behind me. I stared at the wall in front of me, trying to prepare myself for Ella in a cute puffy dress.

"How is she?" A voice asked.

I turned to see Chase. He was sipping some coffee, which was unusual at this time of day. He was probably gearing up for the rescue mission tonight. "She's handling all of this pretty well," I said. "She's exhausted, though. And I don't think she'll be able to rest until she hears from Lindsey again."

"As soon as she's out, we'll put her on the phone so Ella can hear her." Chase glanced back at the door. "I'm guessing she's changing right now. How much did you tell her?"

"I told her everything," I said. "Well, mostly everything."

Chase grinned. "Everything except that you like her, right?"

I scowled at him. He was annoyingly perceptive sometimes. "Her sister is missing. Her apartment got blown up and she almost died because of it. And she's scared of me.

It would be pretty fucked up of me to come on to her right now."

"But it doesn't change your feelings. Blaine told me you spent your poker winnings on her to give her a good-sized commission. And I know you were going to spend that money on renovating your garage."

I shrugged. "It was for a good cause. And again, it doesn't matter. She doesn't want me." She wouldn't ever want any biker. "Just get Lindsey out of there. Please."

"We will. Don't worry. Just keep Ella safe and we'll handle the rest."

There was a tap on the door and I opened it up to see Ella dressed up like a Little. The dress ended halfway down her thighs, leaving her legs bare. Her arms were crossed in front of her chest protectively. She parted her hair into two messy pigtails. She looked at me, biting her lip. "Do I look okay?"

"You look perfect," I said.

Chase cleared his throat, reminding me he was still there. "It's getting dark so you guys can probably leave now. Blaine, Diesel and I are leaving in an hour. As soon as we have Lindsey, we'll call you."

I took off my jacket and handed it to Ella. "Here," I said. "You'll be warmer in this. And old ladies wear the jackets all the time, so it won't look out of place."

She bit her lip. "Can you do me a favor and call me your Little instead of your old lady?" she said. She looked down at the ground. "I know I don't have the right to ask anything after you've done so much for me. But Foghorn called Lindsey his old lady. And I don't really want to think about him."

"Then I won't call you that. I want you to feel comfortable with me. At least as much as you can."

"Thank you."

"You really don't have to thank me for that." Making her comfortable was the least I could do when she was stuck with me for the night. "Come on. Let's go home."

7

Ella

I followed Crowe outside and to his motorcycle. My stomach flip flopped at the thought of riding on it again. All I had felt the first time I rode on it was sheer relief from getting away from the explosion. But for this ride I would actually feel what it felt like to ride on a motorcycle.

Just like earlier, I got on behind Crowe and wrapped my arms around his waist. My bare legs brushed against his rough jeans and now that his jacket was off, only a thin t-shirt separated my hands from his abs. I could feel the heat and the muscles through his shirt. It was scary, but something about it felt tantalizing too.

I was grateful he had given me his jacket. It made me feel a little warmer against the cold night air. He had to be freezing in just a t-shirt, but if he was, he didn't give any indication.

We biked down the road. Crowe went slower this time, but I could still feel the rush of air against my face and legs. Despite my exhaustion, I felt my adrenaline kicking in. In another life, I would have even enjoyed the thrill.

I leaned against Crowe's back and closed my eyes. We biked out of town and to the woods. Soon, there weren't any houses and there was just trees surrounding us. Now I understood why Chase had called Crowe's house a safehouse. It was in the middle of nowhere.

He pulled up in front of a log cabin. With a click of a button, his garage started to open, revealing a messy work area with various motorcycle parts strewn about. He parked his bike inside before closing the garage.

"It's not a lot, but it should be comfortable enough," he said as he led me to the front door. He opened it and stepped aside to let me in.

The heat welcomed me inside. I shivered a little as it hit my bare legs. The front door opened up to a cozy living room with soft, overstuffed couches and a dark green throw rug. An electric fireplace and a flatscreen TV took up one wall that was covered in a red brick facade. There was a bar with barstools that separated the living room from the kitchen. I couldn't see much except for granite countertops and what looked like a gas stove. "Sit down and make yourself comfortable," Crowe said. "I'm sure you're not going to want to go to bed until we hear from Chase."

"No," I said. "Definitely not."

"I'll fix you some tea, then. It'll help warm you up." He went into the kitchen and turned on a kettle while I sat down on the couch. I sank into the soft cushion and felt my body immediately relax as the weariness fell over me like a fog. I barely noticed it as he turned on the electric fireplace or put a soft, warm blanket over me. I struggled to keep my eyes open.

Crowe put a warm mug in my hands. "Drink this," he said. "Come on. For me, baby girl?"

Something about his voice made me feel warm inside. I wanted to please him. He had done so much for me but he hadn't asked for anything in return. Not yet, at least. Nothing should feel good because my sister was missing. But I couldn't help it. Crowe had taken charge as soon as I called him and it was a relief to follow instead of lead for once. I was never good at leading anyway. I was never a good role model. And with Crowe, I didn't have to worry about it. All I had to do was follow his command. Like a good Little.

I sipped the tea. It was peppermint with a hint of chocolate and it tasted amazing. I drank more of it, feeling a little more alert even as it warmed my insides.

Crowe smiled as he watched me. "Good girl."

I smiled and blushed a little before turning away. "Stop," I mumbled.

He swore under his breath, and I tensed up, expecting him to grab me or yell at me. How dare I tell him to stop? After everything he had done for me, I was going to be ungrateful? I prepared myself for the words to come. *Shit. What if he calls Chase and tells him to stop the rescue mission?*

I opened my mouth to apologize, but Crowe beat me to it. "I'm sorry," he said. "I shouldn't have said that. I need to stop making you uncomfortable." He rubbed the back of his neck and stood up. "I can leave you alone if you want."

"No, please stay." I didn't want to be alone. Not right now. "Please. I'm sorry. You're not making me uncomfortable. The opposite, actually." I felt my cheeks burning and I looked down. "It feels good when you call me a good girl. And it felt good when you called me baby girl. But nothing should feel good right now, right? Not when my sister is in trouble."

He knelt next to me and grabbed my hand, gently interlacing his fingers in mine. "You're allowed to feel good, baby girl," he said softly. "You've been through hell. Even before today, you were exhausted and burnt out. I could see it when I entered the store this morning. You deserve a break. And if calling you a good girl makes you happy, then I'll continue to do so. Because you are a good girl. And you deserve kindness."

"I don't know. I feel like I'm a bad sister. She got kidnapped because we fought. If I had just been a better role model or a better provider, then–"

"Hey. Look at me." His voice was firm. I looked around to meet his eyes. He squeezed my hand gently and I realized my hand and the rest of my body was shaking a little. "This is not your fault." He said it so seriously a shiver ran down my spine. "Do you understand, baby girl? None of this is your fault."

I wanted to believe him. I really did. But it was hard.

He cupped my cheek with his hand. His thumb brushed against my bottom lip. "I want to hear you say it," he said. "I want you to tell me that you know this isn't your fault."

"T-this isn't my fault." I swallowed. The words felt wrong and they were hard to get out.

"Again. Say it again."

"This isn't my fault." It was slightly easier to say it this time.

"Good girl." He ran his fingers through my hair as h smiled at me. "Good girl."

Crowe's phone rang, jumping both of us. He grabbed it out of his pocket and answered it before turning away. "Did you get her?"

He listened on the other end and his shoulders slumped forward. My heart started hammering in my chest. They didn't get her. Or maybe she was dead. Fuck. What was I going to do if she was dead? "What's going on?" I whimpered. "What's he saying?"

Crowe turned back to to me, a small smile on his face. He held out the phone to me. "Your sister wants to talk to you."

I snatched the phone out of his hand, barely daring to believe. "Lindsey?"

"Ella?"

A sob escaped me. "Oh my god, you're alive."

"I'm so sorry, Ella. You were right about Foghorn. He's... he's horrible. We're done. I promise."

Part of me wanted to laugh. "I hope so after what he did to you. Are you okay? Where are you?"

"I-I'm okay. I promise. Chase is taking me back to his

place for the night. He said I can stay with him and his old lady until further notice. Our apartment blew up?"

"Y-yeah. It's gone. But we can worry about that tomorrow, okay? You're safe. That's all that matters."

"I love you, Ella."

"I love you too, Lindsey."

As I hung up the phone, something broke inside me and I started crying. Crowe gathered me in his arms and held me tight. "It's okay," he murmured. "It's over now. It's over."

8

Crowe

I held Ella tightly as she cried. Part of me took pleasure in comforting her. The rest of me was disgusted with that part of myself. It still felt like I was taking advantage of her.

But she liked it when I called her a good girl and baby girl. She was willing to be vulnerable around me, even when she was doubting herself. Maybe she wasn't as scared of me now and felt more comfortable around me. She might even start to trust me more.

After several minutes, she had calmed down and was silent. I pulled away slightly to look at her. "Do you want to go to bed now, baby girl? You must be exhausted."

She lifted her face to look at me. In an instant her lips were on mine. I tried to pull back in surprise, but she wrapped her arms around my neck while she kissed me. My cock went hard from kissing her. It felt so good having her tiny body pressed up against mine. Everything about her felt good.

I broke off from the kiss, gasping. "Are you sure, baby girl?" I asked, pushing her hair back from her face. "You've had a hell of a day. You might not be thinking straight right now."

She grabbed my hand and put it against her breast. I could feel its soft heat through the green lace of her dress. "Please, Daddy," she said. "I'm all yours."

I groaned. "You have no idea how good it is to hear you say that." I kissed her as I turned her around and pinned her against my living room rug. I trailed kisses down her neck. "Stop me if I go too far," I said as my hands trailed up her legs. Her legs spread for me, welcoming me.

"Keep going," she whimpered. "Please, Daddy. Keep going."

My cock was so hard. It wanted her so badly. I felt for the cute little diaper she was wearing, and I tore it off her. I thrust a finger into her wet pussy. She pushed against it, wanting more. Unable to resist any longer, I unzipped my pants and pulled out my hard cock. She stared at it with wide eyes. I stroked my cock as I watched her. "Do you like what you see, baby girl?"

She nodded. "Yes, Daddy. Please. Put your cock inside me."

I positioned it at her entrance as I studied her. She bit her lip, looking nervous for a brief second before smiling at me. Fuck, she was gorgeous. I slowly pushed inside her and groaned. Her pussy was so tight.

She whimpered a little as she winced. "Are you okay?" I went to pull out of her.

"No, keep going," she said. "Please, Daddy. It's okay."

"Okay, baby girl." I was positive I had hurt her, but she felt so sweet. Soon, all rational thought left me and I started to thrust in and out of her, groaning. "Fuck, you feel so good, baby girl." I leaned down to claim her mouth with mine as I played with her clit. "Come on my cock," I whispered against her lips. "Come all over Daddy's cock."

She whimpered and moaned as her body started trembling. Soon my teasing was too much for her and she came. Her entire body shook with the orgasm and it was enough to send me over the edge. I gasped and held her tightly as I poured my hot seed into her.

I held her for several seconds as we caught our breath and recovered from our orgasms. Slowly, I pulled out of her. She winced as I did so and my concern came rushing back. "Are you okay, baby girl?" I asked, smoothing her hair away from her face. "Did I hurt you?"

She smiled. "No, Daddy," she said. "That didn't hurt as much as I thought it would, actually."

"What do you mean?" She couldn't possibly be suggesting what I thought she was. Could she?

She cuddled up against me. "This was my first time. But it's okay. I'm glad it was with you."

I swallowed. Fuck. It was her first time and I had taken her like this? I had just fucked her on the floor like an animal. "I'm sorry," I said. "I shouldn't have done that."

"No, don't be sorry."

"You were upset and you've been through hell today.

And I just took advantage of that. I took advantage of you. Fuck. I'm so sorry, baby girl." I held her close, wishing I could go back and change it. I should have gone slower. I should have been more gentle. I should have at least waited until morning when she was more rested.

Ella smiled a little as trailed kisses down my neck. "It's okay. I knew what would happen as soon as I called you. It's okay. I don't mind. I'm yours, Daddy."

I pulled away from her, untangling my body from hers. I felt sick to my stomach. "You were willing to sleep with me to save your sister." I turned away from her. Of course. She still thought I was a monster. She was just willing to let me torture her because she was out of options.

"You can do whatever you want," she said. "It's okay, I promise. I'm yours, Daddy."

"Don't call me that." I stood up and turned away from her. I rested my hands against the bar, closing my eyes. I was an idiot. How did I not see it? That's why she was so curious about being a Little. She wanted to learn how to make me happy. My hands balled up into fists. I should have seen it. Of course she thought I would demand sex. Her landlord just tried to pull that stunt this morning. Foghorn had forced her sister into an "earning opportunity" which boiled down to being forced to have sex with strangers. To her, I'm just another man wanting to exploit her. And I had called her a good girl and baby girl. I thought I was making her feel better, but I probably just made her more scared of me.

"I don't understand," she said, her voice small. "I thought you wanted me."

"I do," I said softly. "But I never wanted to force myself on you. I never wanted to hurt you. And I never, ever expected sex in exchange for finding your sister."

I turned to see her looking at me with wide eyes. She looked completely bewildered. "You were just going to help me?"

"Baby girl... Ella, I was fully prepared to never see you again after helping you find your sister. You never had to play into my fantasies." I took a deep breath, trying to control the swirl of emotions inside me. "Not all bikers are brutes, Ella. I don't take women by force. If I take a Little, it's because she wants it. Not because she thinks she owes me."

Her bottom lip trembled. "I'm sorry," she whispered.

"I'm not mad at you. I'm mad at myself for letting myself go along with it." I sighed. "I wanted it to be true so much, I was willing to turn a blind eye to what should have been obvious." I gave her a smile, but it felt strained. It didn't match any of the emotions inside me. "You should get some sleep," I said. "Take my room. It's down the hall and to the left. There's a lock on the door if it makes you more comfortable."

"No," she said. "You should sleep in your own room."

"I'm not going to be getting much sleep tonight. It's okay. I promise. And in the morning, I'll take you back to town and I'll help you find a new place to live. A place without a piece of shit landlord." And then I would never see her again.

She turned to go down the hall only to turn back. "You're a good man, Crowe," she said. "Probably one of the best men I've ever met. I would have been happy as your Little."

I wanted to believe that. I wanted to be her Daddy. But I couldn't. I wouldn't let myself believe it now. "Sleep well, Ella."

After she disappeared down the hall, I poured myself a shot of whiskey, and then another. I didn't usually drink, but what else could I do? I was in love with a woman who thought I was a monster.

There was no doubt: I was in love with Ella. I wanted her to be mine. I wanted to spoil her and make her laugh and smile. I wanted to dress her up in cute dresses and diapers only to rip them off later. And I wanted to fuck her until she came all over my cock.

But she didn't want me. Not really. And if I was being honest, I didn't deserve her. I should have known what she was thinking. I should have stopped it before I let myself fall into the fantasy. Maybe I gave her my number because I wanted her to be my Little. Did I only help her because I wanted her to be mine?

No. I didn't deserve her. I would never deserve her. I clenched the shot glass in my hand, resisting the urge to throw it across the room.

My phone rang, breaking me out of my thoughts. I grabbed it off the back of the couch. "What?" I barked.

"You fucking bastard," said a voice on the other end. "You're the one who helped the bitch, didn't you?"

I looked at the phone in my hand and realized it was

Ella's phone. The caller ID lit up. Foghorn. I put it against my ear again. "Keep talking. I would love for an excuse to bash someone's brains in right now."

"Then come on out. I'm looking for a fight and a little birdie followed you home from that piece of shit bar."

I looked out my living room window to see a dark figure on a motorcycle. I turned on my outside light and it illuminated a biker. The same biker who tossed a bomb into Ella's window. Now his face was severely bruised. No doubt Chase's handiwork.

He was glaring at me with hatred. I opened my front door and stepped outside. "Get off my fucking property," I said.

"The hell I will," he said, stepping towards me. "You stole my old lady from me. Just because her bitch sister thinks too much of herself–"

I punched him across the face before I could think twice about it. He fell to the ground. I knelt down and grabbed his shirt. "You will never approach them again," I said, punching him in the face. "Even if I have to kill you right now, it'll be worth it if I keep them safe from you." I punched him over and over, until his face was covered in blood and he was coughing.

"Are you fucking crazy?" he choked between blows. "The cops will arrest you. Your life will be a living hell if you kill me. They'll make sure of that."

I didn't doubt him. The cops were so far in the Demon's pocket that they would throw me in jail for the rest of my life. If they didn't just shoot me then and there.

It didn't matter. Nothing mattered except making sure Ella was safe from them.

Why should I care what happened to me? Ella wasn't mine. She would never be mine. I would just be a monster to her.

I heard a shout behind me but I didn't turn to look. I didn't focus on anything except beating Crowe over and over, into a bloody pulp.

Then two tiny hands grabbed mine. "Stop!" Ella cried. "Please."

"Get back inside, Ella," I said. I wasn't going to stop until I finished what I started.

"No! No. I'm not going to let you kill someone. You're better than that."

I snorted. I wasn't better than that. I wasn't better than anything. "Get back inside."

She wrapped her arms around my neck. "Stop, Daddy," she whispered. "Please."

With those words, all of the fight left me. I closed my eyes. "Don't call me that. You don't mean it."

"I do mean it! I want to be your Little, Daddy. Please let me be your Little. Please let me take care of you tonight. Don't go to jail over me. Please."

I couldn't deny her. I sighed and stood up. I picked up Foghorn and tossed him onto the road leading back to town. "Get out of here," I said. "Don't ever come back."

Foghorn was barely conscious, but he started dragging himself down the road, leaving a bloody trail behind him.

Ella tugged on my hand. "Let's go back home, Daddy," she said. "Please."

I followed her into the house. She led me by the hand into the bathroom. "Sit down. I'll clean up your hands."

I looked down. They were covered in blood and bruises. I felt like a monster. "You don't have to," I said. "And you don't have to call me Daddy anymore. You broke me out of the rage."

"I want to call you Daddy," she said. "I meant it. I want to be yours." She grabbed a washcloth and wet it down with hot water.

"You don't mean that, baby– Ella. You don't mean that."

"I do," she said firmly. She started cleaning my hands, wiping off the blood. "I thought I would I have to pretend when I called you. I thought I would hate it and that you would hurt me. But you were so kind and patient with me." She leaned her forehead against mine. "I meant it when I said you were one of the best men I knew. I want to be yours. Please, Daddy, I want to be your Little."

"Oh, baby girl." I shut my eyes, savoring the feeling of having her so close. "I'm yours. I don't know what I did to deserve you, but I promise I'm yours. I'll be your Daddy if that's what you really want. But this time we'll go slow, okay? I want to do it right this time. I want to treat you right."

She smiled and knelt at my feet. She leaned against my leg and closed her eyes. "Okay, Daddy," she said.

I smiled. "Let's get you to bed, baby girl." As I picked her up and carried her into my room, everything felt right. I would do everything I could to make her happy for as long as she truly wanted me to.

VIGOROUS BIKER DADDY

1

Sophie

I stared at the empty storefront in front of me, trying to fight down the panic I was feeling. What the hell was I thinking? I really took out a loan to open up my own business in a mall that was nearly abandoned.

I could smack myself

Unfortunately, there weren't many places in Newbury for businesses to set up. Legitimate businesses, that is. The town was nearly ruined by the Demon biker gang. Even though the Demons lost a lot of their power recently, the town was hanging on by a thread. And the Newbury Mall, as sad as it was, was in the heart of the town.

I took a deep breath, pulled my hair into a ponytail, and got to work unloading the UHaul I had used to bring over my inventory and display cases.

I almost tripped over a crack in the crumbling parking lot and I grimaced. The mall hadn't had the funding to be properly maintained for years. At least the rent was dirt cheap.

I grabbed the first box and pulled it out. It was going to take me at least a couple of hours to unload everything, but at least I wouldn't have to worry about renting the UHaul for more than a day. I was going to need every dollar I could get until I started generating some income.

"Do you need any help with that?" A man asked.

I jumped and took a step back, losing my balance in the process. Strong arms reached out and grabbed me before I fell. "Careful," he said as he helped me to my feet. He grabbed the box which had fallen to the ground. "You okay?" he asked.

I bit my lip. The man seemed kind enough, but he was at least a foot taller than me and built like a wrestler. And he wore a leather jacket. Even though the insignia on it didn't belong to the Demons, it made me nervous all the same. "Yeah, I'm fine," I said, keeping my eyes on the ground. "Thank you."

"No problem. You must be Sophie, right?"

I looked up at him. "How do you know my name?"

He smiled at me. "I'm Ethan. I'm the one who holds your loan."

I took a step back. There was no way I owed money to bikers. "That can't be right," I said. "I got my loan through a program through the mall." The mall was so desperate for business that they started handing out business loans for anyone willing to sign a lease. It was the only way I was able to open up a brick-and-mortar store.

"You're right," he said. "But it was my motorcycle club

who funded the program. So the loan belongs to us. Not the mall."

I swallowed. "Oh."

"It's okay. We're not the Demons. You don't have to be scared."

I looked away. "I'm sorry," I said. "It's just I grew up here. I don't really trust bikers much."

"I understand. Trust me, the Hell's Renegades are the good guys." He gave me a smile. As scary as he looked, the smile softened his face and made him look almost friendly. "So let me help you get unloaded, okay?"

I nodded, not sure what else I could do. I didn't want to piss him off. He held my loan, after all. Sure, it was supposedly through legal methods, but who knew how corrupt the whole program was?

However, I had to admit, everything was faster with Ethan helping me unload the truck. It took barely an hour to finish.

"Do you have anyone else helping you set up, or is it just you?" he asked when I was finished.

"Just me. But I'll manage. Thank you so much for your help."

"Of course." He smiled. "Honestly, I'm just glad more businesses are opening up here. If you need any help, then pop into the Celtic Knot. That's where we hang out. We'll be happy to help you."

I nodded while making a mental note to avoid that place. "Thank you."

After he left, I tried to throw myself into my work. I started setting everything up.

I designed clothes, jewelry, and accessories made out of recycled materials. It was easy to get my hands on old clothing, magazines, and other items destined for landfills. I saved them and gave them new life. It was a lot of fun and I took pride in my work. And I was so excited to be able to have my own brick-and-mortar store to complement my online store. But now that was overshadowed by the fact my loan was owned by a bunch of bikers. If I had known that, I never would have taken the deal.

2

Ethan

After helping Sophie, I went back to the Celtic Knot. Blaine was behind the counter, but it was fairly empty. "Can I have a coffee?" I asked. I needed a caffeine boost before I went to work.

Blaine handed me a cup. "How is the new shop owner settling in?"

I grimaced a little. "She's scared of us but seems nice. She's unpacking now." I sighed.

"Did you tell her we own the loan?"

I shrugged. "Yeah. That was a mistake." I hated that she was scared of us. And I didn't blame her. The Demons were brutal to people who owed them money. Especially if they were pretty young women like Sophie. Even though we had no plans to exploit her, she wouldn't ever believe that.

Blaine sighed. "I told Chase when we started this

program that it had to be more transparent about where the money's coming from."

"Then no one would have taken the loan." I smirked. "We're doing good work here. It'll just take time to gain trust from people."

Blaine snorted. "The Demons ripped apart this town. No one will trust bikers here. Not really."

I was worried he was right about that. But I hoped that wouldn't be true.

Since the Demons showed up on our territory several years ago, the Hell's Renegades has one main mission: destroy them.

The Demons wreaked havoc and destroyed lives wherever they went and it was up to us to fight them off. Eventually, we were able to destroy their headquarters in Newbury and Chase set up a new chapter in Newbury to fight them back.

Unfortunately, the Demons were still around in Newbury. Even though we tried to fight them back, there was only so much we could do with the town so vulnerable. This was why Chase and I approached the mall about a business loan program. I managed the whole operation with club money. We only went through the mall to give it a veneer of respectability to keep us from looking like loan sharks.

The idea was simple: develop a legitimate local economy and people would be less vulnerable to the Demons. However, executing it was easier said than done.

I left the Celtic Knot to go home. The mall offered to give me office space in exchange for the loan program, but

I would be damned if I was working out of an office. Just the thought of it made me feel suffocated.

I had a decent mind for numbers and business, but that didn't come from any sort of office environment. As a teenager, my parents were struggling to make ends meet, so I did the only thing I could think of: I started selling weed.

Eventually, the Hell's Renegades found me and set me straight before I ended up in legal trouble. But it did give me a lot of experience with business and numbers. So I was the natural choice for running a loan program.

I rocked up to my house about half an hour later. It was half of a duplex bordering the outskirts of town. It was a little rundown but it was home.

I opened up my garage and parked my bike inside before I went to the makeshift desk I had set up. I always felt most comfortable in a garage surrounded by bikes, so that's where I kept working.

I spent the day going over loan applications until my vision started to blur. Finally, I stretched, feeling exhausted. I needed a bike ride to relax.

I was putting on my leather jacket when I heard a crash coming from the neighbor's place, followed by shouting.

I frowned. It was probably nothing. Just someone dropping a dish. But my gut told me to check it out anyway.

I went over to the neighbor's front door and knocked on it. "Hey, it's Ethan," I called. "Is everything okay?"

The door opened and I was staring straight in the face

of Reaper, one of the highest-ranking members of the Demon biker gang.

I tensed up immediately and he sneered at me. "What are you doing here?" he said, pushing me back. "You Hell's Renegades can't keep your noses out of other people's business, can you?"

"The better question is what are you doing here?" I said quietly.

He glanced back inside. "I'm just having a chat with my cousin."

I looked over his shoulder to see the tear-stained face of a woman inside. "I don't think your *cousin* wants to have a chat with you."

"It doesn't matter, does it? Either way, it's not your business. Do you want me to call the cops? You know who they'll arrest if I do."

I grimaced. The Demons had the cops in their pockets. I knew exactly who they would believe. But it didn't matter. I wasn't going to let Reaper hurt someone. "Take your little protection racket out of here. She doesn't need your protection."

He sneered. "Doesn't she? Who's going to protect her? You?"

"Maybe." I crossed my arms, daring him to hit me or pull a gun out on me.

Reaper smirked and pulled back his fist. I dodged his first punch, aimed towards my face, but he got me in the stomach. He hit harder than I was expecting and I stumbled back a second, but not before grabbing his shirt and pulling him out of the doorway. I tossed him down on the ground. "Get out of here," I said. "Don't come back."

He grinned at me. "Fine," he said. "I won't. At least right now." He backed away until he reached his bike and then he drove off.

I turned around and went into the doorway. I looked down at my neighbor, whose arms were crossed protectively in front of her face. "Are you okay?" I asked.

She nodded. "Thank you," she said. "I-I'm not his cousin. I don't know why he said that."

"Probably trying to get me to go away without a fight," I said.

"He wanted me to pay him money for protection."

I shook my head. "You don't have to do that," I said. "If he comes back again, then tell me and I"ll take care of it, okay?"

She nodded. "Thank you, Ethan."

"Don't mention it."

I left to go back to my own place. I realized I had left the garage door open in my hurry to make sure my neighbor was all right. And my laptop with all the information about the loan program was gone.

3

Sophie

When I woke up the next day, I couldn't get ready fast enough. I was excited to get back to work in the storefront, setting up displays and getting everything ready for my grand opening in a week.

Despite the nature of my loan, I was hopeful. Even though my brick-and-mortar storefront would probably see only some slow business at first, it would grow with time. And luckily my online store was busy enough. I'll just have to focus on paying off the loan as soon as possible so I wouldn't be indebted to a bunch of bikers. I could do it.

I went to my store, ready to get to work. But I stopped as soon as I saw it. The glass windows were shattered and the inside was completely trashed. Clothing and furniture were torn to bits and tossed on top of each other in a tangle of kindling and cloth. The stench of bleach stung my nose as I looked at what used to be a pile of colorful skirts and dresses made from old table cloths that were now streaked white.

On the counter was a display of elaborate necklaces and earrings I had made from paper beads. I had spent hours rolling strips of junk mail catalogues into bead shapes and then sealing it into place with glossy glue. I was able to make intricate and flashy designs with them because they were so lightweight.

Now all of them were sitting in a puddle of water in front of the counter. The beads had dissolved into mush. The back wall had the Demon's insignia spray-painted onto it in blood red.

I stood for a second in the doorway of my store, stunned. This had to be a nightmare. This couldn't be real. How could this have happened? Everything was fine when I went home late last night.

I didn't know how long I spent staring at the ruins that used to be my store. I had no idea what my next step would be. I couldn't go to the police. The Demons had them in their pocket. Everyone knew that. But I didn't know what I was going to do. I had brought my entire inventory here and it was gone. It would take weeks if not months to build it back up, not to mention I had to clean it all up and buy more furniture to get it even close to presentable.

My face felt hot and I realized I was crying. I closed my eyes as I sobbed. How the hell was I going to make this okay?

I barely heard voices from behind me.

"She's here."

"Holy shit!"

I turned to see two men in leather jackets running towards me. On reflex, I covered my head with my arms. "Don't!"

"It's okay, Sophie," one of them said. "It's me, Ethan. Remember me from yesterday?"

I looked up at him. He was kneeling in front of me, his brow furrowed in concern. "I'm sorry," I whispered. "I'm going to fix this. I'll pay back the loan on time. I promise."

His jaw clenched. "Don't worry about that right now. Are you okay? Did they hurt you?"

I shook my head. "I never even saw them."

The other biker peered inside my store. "They were thorough," he said.

I looked between Ethan and the other biker. "How did you guys know the Demons were here?"

Ethan's expression darkened. "I fucked up. Plain and simple."

"You did what you needed to do," the other biker said. He looked at me. "I'm Chase, by the way. I'm the club president."

"I-It's nice to meet you," I said. I was still confused on how Ethan would have caused this. And even though Ethan told me not to worry about the loan right now, my stomach still lurched at the club president seeing my store in this case.

"Ethan, help her clean up this mess and protect her in case they come back. We'll deal with the rest." Chase said.

I looked up at him. "Protect– no, please. I'm okay. I promise." I remembered when I was a kid and watched my parents scrimp and save only to hand all of their money to the Demons for protection. If they didn't give enough then we would wake up with bricks thrown through our windows and the locks busted off our doors. I couldn't be afford protection.

"You're not okay," Ethan said. "Because of me, you're in danger. The least I can do is protect you."

"We don't charge for protection," Chase said. "We're not the Demons. And they could come back. We're not sure."

I bit my lip and nodded. I hated it but he was right. I didn't know the Hell's Renegades, but the Demons were bad news.

Chase left me and Ethan together. Ethan turned to me. "I'm so sorry, Sophie."

"I don't see how this is your fault," I said.

His jaw clenched and he looked away. "I had the information for the loan program at my house. I'm not sure how the Demons knew that, but they did. Last night they distracted me and stole my laptop. Now you and the other loan applicants are in danger."

I frowned. "Why would they care about some random stores opening up in the mall?"

"Because they thrive on instability," said Ethan. "Towns rebuilding their communities and economies are less vulnerable. Less people joining the Demons, less desperate people buying their drugs and going to their brothels to escape their depressing lives." He sighed. "I should have known they would pull a stunt like this."

I looked at my ruined store. "I guess I should get to work cleaning," I said.

"I'll help you." He pushed up the sleeves of his leather jacket. "Just let me know where to start."

"You really don't–"

"I really do." He gave me a look that sent shivers down my spine.

I looked away. "O-okay. I guess you can start with trying to remove the spray paint. I need to sort through the mess and see if any of it is salvageable."

Luckily, my cleaning supplies was below the counter and appeared to be untouched. I handed a Ethan a bucket and cleaning rags and I grabbed gloves and a trash bag for myself.

We worked in silence with him trying to scrub off the insignia with a glower on his face and me picking through the debris on the ground, looking for anything at all that was salvageable.

I tried not to cry as I put pieces of display tables into the trash bag, only to find ruined clothing beneath it. Clothing I had worked so hard on. What a waste.

I didn't get far before I felt tears run down my face. I tried to block it out but my breath started growing fast as panic rose up inside of me. I collapsed on the ground and covered my face with my hands, sobbing.

"Sophie. Hey." Ethan whispered in my ear. I barely heard him. I couldn't stop crying.

He pulled me into his arms and rubbed my back. "It's okay," he said. "It's going to be okay."

He kept whispering comforting words in my ear as I cried. Slowly I calmed down. Ethan pulled away from me when I stopped crying. He looked down at me, the concern obvious in his eyes. "Let's take a break," he said.

I nodded numbly. A break wouldn't hurt.

4

Ethan

I hated seeing Sophie like this. She looked so broken and sad. I couldn't even imagine how soul-crushing it would be to see everything she had worked for to be destroyed like that. When I sold marijuana, I worried more about a fire taking all of my inventory more than getting caught my the cops. And even though I prided myself on growing good quality plants, that wasn't anything compared to the time and love Sophie had put in each piece of clothing.

I wished I could take her to the Celtic Knot. That place was always like a sanctuary for me in this godforsaken town. But they were closed for the day and the club members were scattered to the winds trying to protect everyone attached to the loan program. Chase was also taking a couple of club members to retaliate against the Demons and get the laptop back. After today, any information about the loan program will stay locked in Chase's office at the end of the day.

I took Sophie to the food court. It was pretty sad, with only a couple of small fast food places hanging on for dear life. I ordered her to sit down at a table while I got some food from the Chinese takeout restaurant.

She obeyed automatically. I tried not to think about the rush of pleasure I felt by her obeying me so quickly like that. I enjoyed it way too much.

I couldn't help it. Something about her brought out the Daddy instincts inside of me. I felt protective of her. She felt so small and vulnerable. But I had to be careful. I didn't even know if she was a Little or not. And even if she was, she wouldn't want a biker like me as her Daddy. She was scared of me and the only reason why she was putting up with me was in case the Demons came back.

I set down trays of Chinese food on the table along with a cardboard cup of hot tea. "This might help," I said.

She nodded. "Thank you," she said. Her voice was rough and scratchy. "I'm sorry. I shouldn't have broken down like that in front of you."

"Crying is healthy," I said. "Your entire life got turned upside down. You have a right to cry."

"I don't know what I'm going to do," she said. "I mean I have a lot of supplies still at my house, but I brought all of my inventory here. I'm going to have to build everything back up." She sighed. "And it's such a waste. I like upcycling old products to cut down on waste. So this makes it seem so much worse." She sipped her tea. Just a sip made her look so much more relaxed.

I wished I knew of a way to make her feel better. But I was at a loss for everything. "How about after food, I take you back to your place?" I asked. "I understand if you don't want me to come inside. But you can grab what you need to create and you can work on that while I clean up."

She bit her lip. "I'm not sure. That's a lot of work for you to do by yourself."

"It's the least I can do. It's my fault you're in this mess in the first place. Besides, there's a lot of broken glass from the windows. I don't want you to get hurt."

Sophie nodded. "Okay. Just... if you see anything that doesn't look completely shredded, can you save it? I want to salvage as much as I can."

"Yeah, of course."

After eating, we went to Sophie's car in the parking lot. I looked around, keeping an eye out for any unknown motorcycles or anyone in the parking lot, but there wasn't anyone except us. The mall's lot was depressingly empty except a couple of cars that probably belonged to employees of the remaining businesses.

We drove to Sophie's house. It was a modest one-story house surrounded by a tall picket fence. I raised an eyebrow at the fence. "You fulfilling childhood dreams of living in a fortress or something?"

She blushed a little. "I know it's silly but it makes me feel safer. It makes me feel like I'm blocking out the rest of Newbury."

I nodded. "I understand. It's important to feel safe in your own home. And it's smart in a town like this."

I waited in the car while she ran inside to get supplies.

I wanted to follow her and help her. I also felt antsy letting her out of my sight. But I didn't want to intrude. She was scared of me and her home was her safe space. I didn't want to ruin that.

A few minutes later she came out with a plastic storage bin full of items. I glanced in the back and saw on top of it was a teddy bear made out of patchwork fabric. I couldn't help but feel drawn to it. Maybe she was a Little after all. It looked like it had been finished, after all. And she said her entire inventory was at the shop...

No. I couldn't think like that. It was none of my business if she was a Little or not.

We pulled into the mall parking lot again. I insisted on carrying Sophie's supplies for her. It was the least I could do, after all.

Back in the store, she started to set up a makeshift work area on the sales counter with a small sewing machine and what looked like a pile of ragged clothing that had seen better days.

I went back to cleaning the Demon insignia off the wall. Before anything else, I wanted that gone. I didn't want that hanging over our heads like a brand.

Sophie seemed to visibly relax as she started to sew. I was happy about that. It was nice seeing how much she cared about her work. She clearly enjoyed it a lot. I just hoped she would be able to recover from the Demon's attack okay.

We spent the rest of the day working in almost complete silence. Sophie was absorbed into her work and

I didn't want to distract her. After I washed off the spray paint, I started to pick through the debris on the ground.

The Demons had done a really good job of destroying everything within sight. Most of the clothing was just ragged strips covered in splinters and gross water and bleach. I found a couple of small purses and a belt that were mostly intact but aside from that, everything had to go in the trash.

I was glad I was the one picking it up and not Sophie. It was painful looking at the pieces of quilts and dresses and skirts on the ground, obviously crafted with love. I couldn't imagine how hard it would be for Sophie to pick them up.

I paused when I found a pile of mutilated teddy bears. Their insides were ripped out and their heads were ripped off. I looked at them uncertainly. I found one that was mostly intact aside from its head and one of its leg ripped off. "Do you think these are worth saving?" I asked, holding it up.

She looked at it and flinched before looking down. "If they weren't sprayed with bleach or filthy water \then might as well," she said. "Those look a little more salvageable."

I put them into a pile and ran my hands through a tangle of threads and tiny pieces of fabric. "I'm not sure where this came from," I said. "It looks like they ran something through the shredder."

"Oh that came from the bears. I save the scraps of fabric too small to work with and use it as stuffing."

"That's really smart."

She shrugged but gave a small smile. "I just don't like waste." She blushed. "But I do like teddy bears. They're not a big seller but they're fun to make."

I smiled warmly. "If they're fun to make, then that's all that matters."

After another hour of working, Chase came back. He looked exhausted and he had a black eye. His knuckles were bruised and cut. I knew he had beaten someone to shit. "I've got good news and bad news," he said. "I got the laptop back. But it's smashed to shit." He smiled grimly. "I smashed their computers to shit in return after wiping their serves clean. We were planning to blow the place, but we got ambushed before we had the chance. Got our asses kicked, but they shouldn't have the information for the loan program anymore."

"Good," I said. "What's the next step?"

Chase surveyed the shattered store windows with a critical eye. "The next step paying for this place to get fixed up somehow. I'll have to ask the other club presidents for help, but we'll make it work. Maybe Hawk knows a repair man who owes him."

Hawk was one of our first club presidents. He had chased the Demons out of his territory before they were able to put down roots. He ran some poker games in his bar for a little extra income. Now and then people owed him money. Maybe we'd get lucky and he would be able to call in a favor.

Sophie looked up from her work. "You really don't have to do that," she said. "I-I can't really afford to increase my debt to you. It might take me longer than I expected to open but I'll make it work."

"This is our fault," Chase said. "We clean up our own messes. And you can consider your loan forgiven. Ethan will get it in writing by the end of the week."

I nodded, satisfied with that.

Sophie looked completely bewildered. "I don't understand," she said. "Why would you forgive the loan?"

"We didn't create the loan program to take advantage of people," I said. "We did it to help. And right now the only way to help you is to forgive the loan." It would set the program back a little, but that was okay. We would make it work.

She looked down, blushing. "I don't know what to say."

"You don't have to say anything," Chase said. He looked at a ragged t shirt I had set aside. It was mostly intact aside from some bleach stains. He smirked. "But if you take custom orders, my old lady would love some dresses made by you."

5

Sophie

I couldn't believe the Hell's Renegades were being so nice. I was so worried about paying back their loan with all of my inventory ruined and they were happy to help just like that. I could barely believe it.

After the day was over, Ethan had cleaned up the majority of the mess. Aside from the teddy bears, he had found a few items of clothing worth saving. It was a paltry inventory, but at least not everything was lost.

I had finished a dress I had started a couple of days ago along with a few headbands and a belt. I was in the process of making a clutch purse now. I decided to focus on making a lot of accessories because they were quicker to make and they sold faster online. Even with my loan forgiven, the sooner I could rebuild my income, the better.

At the end of the day, I slowly packed up my sewing. Ethan was still with me, carefully putting pieces of teddy bear into a trash bag for me to take home and sort through. I didn't know what to do. Was he planning on coming home with me? "So, Chase made it sound like the mission was a success," I said. "He got the information back. The Demons probably won't attack me again, right?"

"He's calling for backup from the other club chapters," Ethan said. "They'll attack enough to hurt. It'll keep them licking their wounds for awhile. And someone will now be constantly watching the mall in case of an attack. So it's unlikely they'll come after you again."

I bit my lip. The Hell's Reneages were definitely efficient at holding off the Demons. "So you don't have to watch me anymore. Do you?"

He fixed me with a state as if he was trying to figure out what I was thinking.

"I mean, you must have better things to do than just babysit me."

"Do you want me to leave?" he asked.

Slowly, I shook my head. "No," I admitted.

"Then I won't leave," he said gently. "If I make you feel safer, then I want to stay."

He did make me feel safe. I never thought I would see the day when a biker made me feel safe, but here I was. Ethan was so patient and kind. Unlike any biker I had ever known.

"Please stay," I whispered."

"I will. I promise." He gave me a kind, gentle smile. "It's okay. You're okay with me."

I believed him.

He was willing to spend the night at my place. I felt a

flutter of nerves as I got into my car, him following me on his bike. It was going to be the first time a man had ever been in my home.

Growing up, my parents forbid me from dating. They were too scared I would end up with someone who was really kidnapping girls for the Demons. I didn't have enough time to date anyway. I was too busy working afterschool and weekends to help them make ends meet. I also needed time for my sewing projects.

Even though I moved out by myself and managed to make upcycling my full time job, I still never had enough time to date.

So this would be the first time a man had been in my house. Even though it was platonic-- I doubted Ethan would even want me after I broke down like that in front of him-- I couldn't help but feel a little nervous anyway.

I pulled into my driveway and went to grab my things from the back. Ethan pulled up right behind me, the roar of the motorcycle dying as he parked. "Let me help you with that," he said.

I grabbed the bag of teddy bears. ""Thanks but I have it." I tried to pick up the storage bin, but it was heavy.

He gently grabbed it from me. "You don't have to do everything by yourself," he said. "I'm here to help."

"You've already helped a lot."

"Not nearly enough."

I started walking to the house. "You don't have to beat yourself up over this," I said. "It's not your fault the Demons hurt you like that."

"Yes, it is," he said. "It's my fault."

"The Demons suck," I said. "They'll find any way they can to hurt someone. I wouldn't be surprised if they trashed my store sooner or later even if they didn't get the information about the loan program."

His expression remained moody. "I still hate that I put you at risk."

"Now you're helping me rebuild and protecting me," I said. "There isn't anything more I could ask for."

I led him inside my house. Luckily, I kept it fairly clean and organized. I had decorated the walls with patchwork quilts I had made from bigger scraps. It gave splashes of color throughout the house and filled it with a nice comforting feeling. On the couch were a couple of patchwork teddy bears. I liked hugging the teddy bears. It might be childish but it made me feel safe.

Instead of a guest room, I had a sewing room on one side, where I made most of my clothing. But in the living room on the coffee table was a tray will all of my bead making and jewelry making supplies because it was easier to make those while watching TV.

"Make yourself at home," I said. "Do you want any tea or water?"

"I'll get it," he said. "Have a seat and relax."

I smirked. "I don't really relax," I said. "I just kind of keep working until I need to sleep."

He raised an eyebrow. "All the more reason to relax. Sit down. I'll get you some water. And maybe something to eat."

I relented and sat down in the living room. I opened up the bag teddy bear parts and I was in the middle of restuffing a teddy bear head when Ethan sat a glass of water down on the table in front of me. "I told you to relax. Not keep working. You've already done a lot of work today."

"I can't help it," I said. "I have a lot of catching up to do."

He gently took the bear away from me. "You've had a long day and you've worked all day. You need to relax more than anything."

I made a face but I knew he was right. My hands were aching from all of the sewing and my entire body felt stiff.

But I still itched to start working again. I couldn't help it, not when there was so much to do. But I knew he was right. I needed a break.

I turned on the TV and tried to relax while drinking my water. I ended up turning on a kid's movie. They always made me kind of happy. It was silly. I was an adult after all and should act like it. But kid movies were just happier than movies for adults.

A little while later, Ethan came in with two plates of food. He had fried up some chicken and served it with a side of mixed vegetables from a frozen vegetable medley I had in the freezer. "It's not much," he said. "But I didn't want to poke around your kitchen too much."

"You wouldn't have found much more than this anyway," I said. "I'm not much of a cook." I smiled and took a bite of the chicken. "This is so good," I said. I quickly took another bite.

He chuckled. "I love to good but it's not often I get to

cook for someone besides myself. So I'm happy you like it."

I looked up at him with wonder. "You're unlike any biker I've ever known," I said.

"I hope that's a good thing."

I nodded and looked down at the food. "Definitely. The Demons made my parents pay for protection. Everything we had went to paying them off. But as the years went on, they kept increasing the price even though they had to know we wouldn't be able to pay it."

"They were counting on it," Ethan said. His jaw clenched. "I'm guessing they got even more aggressive when you turned eighteen."

"How did you know?"

"They especially like to target cute young girls for their brothels," he said. "I'm sure they wanted to get their hands on you any way they could. If they outright kidnapped you then your parents would have made too much noise trying to find you. But if they bully your parents into giving you up to protect themselves then there wouldn't be any noise."

I shuddered. "They actually kidnapped women that way?"

"Too many of them. They also steal them off the street but it's harder for them to get a hold of women with loving families. That's why they tried to break you guys down."

I curled up into a ball on the couch. "I'm glad my parents fought for me," I said. "I wonder if they knew."

"Where are your parents now?"

"When the Demons' headquarters were destroyed,

they took their chance to move out of Newbury. But I stayed behind. I had always wanted to own my own house and real estate is cheap here."

"Yeah, I'm sure," he said dryly.

"Are you from Newbury?"

"No, thank god. Otherwise I might have ended up with the Demons instead of the Hell's Renegades. I grew up in Hawk's territory. He's another club president. He found me when I was a snarky, dumbass kid. He kept me from selling weed to an undercover cop and offered to help me. I needed to help my parents make ends meet and Hawk was willing to help me out to keep me from being arrested. I sold weed under him for awhile and then ran some of the poker games in his territory. But it became obvious my talent lied in handling money. Eventually I moved here to help Chase in Newbury. That's how I ended up managing the loan program."

I frowned. "The Hell's Renegades sells marijuana and runs poker games?"

"They don't really sell weed anymore, but they still run games. But that only happens in Hawk's and Dante's branches. There are too many dirty cops here for Chase to do that. They're itching for a reason to get rid of us."

"So that's why you did the loan program." I know it was mainly to help people, but there was an interest rate on the loan. It was more reasonable than any loan through the bank, but it was still there.

Ethan nodded. "We mainly did it to hurt the Demons and help Newbury. But a little extra income in addition to the Celtic Knot wouldn't hurt."

He smiled at me, suddenly looking a little tired. "But you don't have to worry about that. Come on. You should probably get to bed before it gets too late."

As if on cue, I yawned. "I still need to make up the couch for you. Will you be able to even fit on it?" I looked at him skeptically. He was so big it was hard to imagine he would be able to sleep comfortably.

He smiled. "Don't worry about me. I can sleep anywhere. All I need is a pillow and a blanket."

I went to my linen closet next to the bathroom and pulled out a quilt and a pillow. I handed it to him. "I hope this will work."

He smiled as he looked at the patchwork quilt. "Where do you find the time to make all of these?" he asked. "I can believe you don't get sewed out after working all day on your inventory."

I smiled. "I like making quilts. And I made these when I was still learning. They're not nearly as nice as the ones I sell."

He ran his hand over one of the patches, which was fraying a little on one of the seams. I made a mental note to repair it when I got a chance. Whenever that may be. "I don't know," he said. "This looks pretty good to me."

I smiled. "Well I'm glad you like it. I hope you manage to get some sleep."

"I'm sure I will. I hope you sleep well too, little one." He flinched and looked away. "Shit. I'm sorry. I didn't mean to say that."

I felt my cheeks burn a little even as my stomach fluttered. "Don't be sorry," I said. "I enjoyed that. I don't know... it made me feel safe."

His gaze heated up. "Good," he said. "I want to make you feel safe. Little one."

I bit my lip and looked down. "Goodnight," I squeaked before running to my room.

6

Ethan

I couldn't believe I made her feel safe. Even better, she felt safe when I called her little one. I hadn't meant to but she looked so adorable and sweet and it had just slipped out.

Luckily she didn't seem to mind too much. I liked making her feel safe. I wanted her to feel safe when she was with me.

I ended up spreading out on the floor instead of the couch which was way too small for me. It wasn't the most comfortable but I would manage.

I might have exaggerated my ability to sleep anywhere. I used to be able to do that. But now I was almost thirty and sleeping on the floor would definitely give me a backache the next morning. It was more than worth it if Sophie felt safe.

I thought back to what she had told me about her childhood. No wonder she needed to feel safe now. She had lived in fear of the Demons taking her home from her her entire life. She was lucky her parents cared enough to fight for her. I knew too many woman whose parents sold them to save their own hides.

I would do everything I could to protect her now. I didn't want her hurt. Just the thought of the Demons touching her made me clench my fists with anger.

I closed my eyes and tried to go to sleep. Eventually I managed to doze a little only to be woken up by the sound of someone crying.

I woke up fully and went to Sophie's bedroom door. I heard the sound of her sobbing inside. I tapped lightly on the door. "Sophie, are you okay?" I asked.

She didn't answer.

Slowly, I opened the door and let myself in. She was curled up in bed, hugging a teddy. It looked like she was crying in her sleep.

I debated whether to just let her be or wake her up. After all, I might scare her by suddenly appearing in her room like this. But I didn't want to leave her trapped in whatever nightmare was making her cry like that. Just the thought of it made my heart ache.

I sat down on the edge of the bed and slowly shook her awake. "Sophie, wake up," I said. "It's all right. You're safe now."

Her eyes slowly fluttered open. "Ethan?"" she said. Her voice was small and high-pitched, like a Little's. I stifled a groan.

"I'm here, little one," I said. "You were crying in your sleep."

"I'm sorry. I didn't mean to wake you."

"I'm glad you did." I brushed away some of her tears. "What were you dreaming about?"

"I dreamed about the Demons coming for me." She shuddered. "Them breaking into my store again and grabbing me and.... killing you."

I was surprised I had entered her dream at all, but I couldn't help but feel a little touched. I gathered her up in my arms, enjoying the way her tiny body fit against mine. "They couldn't kill me if they tried," I said. "I'm not going anywhere, little one. I promise. And I'll never let them take you."

"How can you be so sure?" she whispered.

"Because I'm stronger than them. The Hell's Renegades are stronger than them. And it'll do whatever it takes to keep you safe. I promise."

She buried her face in my chest. "Can you stay with me tonight?" she asked, her voice small. "It's okay if you don't want to."

"Yes, little one," I said. "I'm happy to stay with you." I couldn't believe my luck. I wished it was under better circumstances,k but I was so happy I would be able to hold her for the night.

I got under the covers with her and she curled her body around mine. I turned her teddy bear under her arm. "Can't forget this little guy," I said.

She blushed a little. "You must think I'm so childish."

"Not at all, little one," I said. "You're so brave and strong and smart. There's nothing wrong with having a stuffy to keep you company."

She bit her lip as she looked up at me. "Really?"

"Really, little one." I stroked her hair as I looked down at her. I wanted to kiss her so badly. But I resisted that urge. She needed comfort. Not some biker taking advantage of her. "Try to sleep, little one."

"Yes, D-- yes."

My blood heated up immediately at her words. Because if I didn't know any better, I would assume she was about to call me Daddy.

7

Sophie

I woke up the next morning to the scent of bacon and eggs wafting into my bedroom from the kitchen. Ethan was gone, but there was a cup of English breakfast tea on my nightstand. I smiled as I sipped it. He was so sweet.

I blushed a little as I remembered last night. What was I thinking inviting him into bed with me? He probably felt so uncomfortable about it.

But he was so strong and protective. He reminded me of the love interests in romance novels. Romance novels were a guilty pleasure of mine, especially ones with DDLG themes. I wasn't sure why, but I liked the idea of a big, strong Daddy taking care of me.

Before last night, it never occurred to me to think of Ethan in that way. Sure he was sexy, but he was also scary. Not to mention he was a biker. But this past day he had been so patient and nice. Last night, when he held me and comforted me, he didn't seem scary at all. He didn't even mind that I slept with a teddy bear. I had always been worried that would freak out any man I would bring home, but Ethan didn't seem to mind at all.

I sipped my tea as I left my room. I found Etlhan in the kitchen, frying up bacon and eggs. He turned and smiled at me as I entered. "Good morning," he said, giving me a sleepy smile. "Breakfast is almost ready."

I smiled and sat down at the table. "This looks fantastic," I said. "Thank you so much."

"It's my pleasure, little one," he said. I felt warm inside at the nickname again.

"Do you have to go to work today?" I asked.

He looked at me and then nodded slowly. "I need to get back to work. But I'm going to be in the Celtic Knot if you need me. It's not very far from your shop."

I smiled and nodded. "I'm glad you'll be close by," I said.

He looked uncertain. "If you want me to stay with you, I can make it work."

"No," I said quickly. I gave him a soft smile. "No. But thank you. You need to get to work. I'm just going to be sewing anyway. Maybe I'll listen to some music or something while I work."

He nodded. "That's a good idea."

After breakfast, I drove to the mall again with him following behind me. I lugged all of my sewing supplies inside. Even though Ethan assured me a biker would be watching the mall in case the Demons attacked again, I didn't want to leave my things there overnight. At least not until my windows were repaired.

The shop was still messy, but Ethan had done a good job of cleaning up most of it. The only things left was mopping and sweeping. Then I would have to buy displays and clothing racks again. I wondered how customers would react if I just had cheap folding tables spread out, like a yard sale. I smiled grimly at the thought. It wasn't ideal but it would get me open that much sooner.

I set up everything on the counter and I put on music, a playlist of Disney songs. Soon I was singing along as I stitched up some mangled teddy bears.

They weren't the most pretty looking. I had to add a lot of extra seams to hold them together. But they were still soft and squishy.

Honestly, I was happy I got to save these. The thought of tossing out teddy bears was so sad, even if they had gotten ripped apart. But stitching them back together felt cathartic.

I was so focused on my work that I didn't notice Ethan enter until he was almost right beside me. I looked up and smiled, feeling myself blush at the same time. "Hi," I said shyly.

"Hey, little one," he said. "You ready to take a break?"

I looked at the pile of teddy bears I had left. "I don't have time for a break."

"Yes you do. Come on."

I hesitated. I wasn't sure about this. "I really don't have the time. I want to get several more of these sewn up.

"I'm not giving you a choice," he said. "I'm not going to

let you exhaust yourself like this. You need food and a break."

"I don't feel for food court food."

He grinned. "I'm not taking you to the food court today." Ethan grabbed my hand and led me out of the shop. Instead of taking me to the food court, he took me to the Celtic Knot. I stopped in my tracks when I looked inside. Several bikers were inside, eating and drinking even though it was early afternoon. There were a few women flitting about in minidresses and overalls, acting as if a biker bar was the safest back in the world. But nerves fluttered in my stomach anyway.

"It's okay," Ethan said. "No one will hurt you here. I promise. They're all Hell's Renegade members."

I slowly nodded. I trusted Ethan. I knew he wouldn't put me in a dangerous situation.

Ethan led me into the pub. There were a few glances, but not many people spared us many looks. A young woman was tending the bar. She was dressed in a cute barmaid outfit, her hair done up in pig tails. She grinned when she saw us. "Hi Ethan!" she said, sounding genuinely excited to see him. She turned to me and stuck out her hand. "Hi, I'm Hannah. You must be Sophie. I've heard a lot about you."

I shook her hand hesitantly. "You have?"

She nodded. "Ethan's talked a lot about you."

Ethan rolled his eyes. "I may have mentioned you a few times," he said. "Hannah, can you get us both some sandwiches please?"

She nodded. "Right away!" She flitted into the kitchen

as if she was a woodland fairy. Her skirt flew up for a second and I could have sworn I saw her wearing a diaper. But that had to have been my imagination.

I couldn't help but be envious of her energy. "Hannah seems nice," I said. "Is she the only bartender here?"

"Blaise, her Daddy, is here too. He's the chef and he also tends the bar. But because it's so busy, she's up front so he can focus on the food."

"Her Daddy? You mean her father?" I couldn't imagine any of these bikers even knowing about DDLG, let alone being into it. They seems way to rough and tough for that.

But Ethan shifted uncomfortably on his barstool. "No, little one," he said. "Not her father. The Hell's Renegades have a certain type with what they like in a romantic partner."

He was interrupted by a woman coming up from behind us. "Hi!" she said, plopping down on the stool next to me on my other side. "I'm Melody, I'm Chase's old lady. You must be Sophie. It's nice to meet you." She hugged a stuffy tight to her chest and I knew what Ethan meant. The Hell's Renegades were really all Daddys. Did that mean... was Ethan a Daddy too?

I shook those thoughts out of my mind. Even if he was a Daddy, that didn't mean he wanted me as a Little. I focused on Melody. "Hi," I said shyly. "I like your stuffy."

She beamed at me. "I like your dress. Did you make it yourself?"

I looked down at patchwork dress I had made out of scraps of blue and green fabric. I loved it because it made me feel like a fairy princess. "Yes," I said. "I'm actually opening up a store in the mall."

She practically bounced in her seat. "I'm so excited for that!" she said. "We all are. Do you do custom orders? I would love for you to make me a dress just like yours."

I nodded. "I'd be happy to." I bit my lip. "I also make teddy bears, i-if you want one of those as well."

Her eyes widened. "You do?"

Ethan chuckled from behind me. "I'll leave you two be," he said. "I have a feeling you guys will have a lot to talk about."

We talked about teddy bears and clothing for the rest of lunch. When Hannah came back with the food, she joined the conversation. Soon a lot of the women were surrounding me. All of them wanted a teddy bear and several of them also wanted dresses. They were all so nice and sweet too.

I could barely believe it. By the time lunch was over, I had orders for six dresses and ten teddy bears. Not only would it keep me busy, but it would give me enough income to tide me over while I rebuilt my inventory.

Ethan walked me back to my stop after lunch. "I hope they weren't too much," he said. "They get excited when they find another Little." He glanced at me, as if judging my reaction.

I felt myself blush. "Is it that obvious?" I asked.

He grinned. "Not at first. I was really only certain over lunch when I was watching you with th others."

I looked down. "I don't know much about it to be honest," I said. "I've never been with a Daddy before. For that matter, I've never been with anyone. But I've read books about it and I know it makes me feel good."

"It makes you feel safe, doesn't it?"

I nodded.

He looked at me a little wistfully. "I got to admit I want to be your Daddy, little one. You're so cute and sweet. But I understand if you don't want a biker for a Daddy. I won't mention it again if you say so."

I blushed and looked down. "I... I want you to be my Daddy."

He groaned softly and grabbed my hand, his fingers intertwining with mine. "You just made my day, little one."

I felt my stomach flutter and I looked up at him nervously. "I-I still don't know how to be a Little. I don't know how to be good or how to make you happy–"

"Shh." He grabbed my chin and raised my head to make me look at him. "Listen to me because I'm only going to say this once. You'll never disappoint me or make me angry. All you have to do is be yourself and follow any rules I give you. That's all. And from what I've seen, you're a perfect Little."

8

Ethan

I took Sophie back to her place that night after work. She was tired, so I decided to leave my bike at the mall and drive her back myself in her car. She dozed against the car window, looking more related than I've ever seen her. A slight smile graced her lips, which made me grin. She looked so adorable. It made me unbelievably happy that she could be so relaxed with me.

We rocked up to her driveway and I put my hand on her arm. "Come on, little one," I said. "We're home."

She sighed and her eyes fluttered open before she stretched and yawned. "I'm sleepy, Daddy."

Fuck, she sounded so good saying that.

"Let's get you inside. You need to eat something before bed."

Her nose wrinkled up in distaste. "I'm not hungry."

"You just have to eat a little." I got out of the car and

went around to the other side to open it for her. She got out and I led her into the house.

She sat down at the kitchen table and I opened up her freezer. I pulled out some thin steak strips and french fries. "How does steak sandwhiches sound?"

"That sounds perfect, Daddy."

I smiled. "Good girl." I tossed the fries into the oven before cooking up the steak. It didn't take more than half an hour to make the entire meal.

I served it to her and watched her eat it eagerly. I smirked. So much for not being hungry.

After we finished eating, Sophie seemed a lot more alert than before. "I think I can work a little before bed," she said.

"Oh no, you don't," I said. I picked her up and tossed her over my shoulder which made her shriek with giggles.

I took her to her bedroom and set her gently on the bed. "You've been working all day, little one," I said. "It's time for you to relax. If you don't want to go to bed I could read a story to you."

She nodded. "That sounds perfect, Daddy. I have some children's books under the bed."

I smiled and looked under the bed to find a small storage bin with children's books. I chose a beginner chapter book.

"All right," I said, settling on the bed next to her. I grabbed her teddy bear from the nightstand and handed it to her. She hugged it to her chest while I opened up the book. Sophie cuddled up against me as I read aloud to her. Several chapters in, a realized she was looking up at me. And she wasn't looking the least bit tired. "Having fun, little one?" I asked.

She nodded and then bit her lip. "Can I kiss you, Daddy?" she asked.

My blood heated up at the suggestion. "Yes little one," I said. My voice was hoarse. "If that's what you want."

She tilted her face up to meet mine as my lips met hers. Her lips were soft and plump. I groaned softly as I melted into the kiss. "You taste so sweet, little one," I said.

She smiled and crawled into my lap so she was straddling me. I groaned, feeling my cock harden. I kissed her again. Her arms wrapped around my neck and I put my arms around her waist.

Her tongue darted out to lick my lower lip and I groaned and pulled away. She looked up at me, uncertain. "Did I do something wrong?"

"Of course not, little one. You're perfect. But if we keep going, I'm not going to be able to stop myself." I brushed a stray hair out of her face. "I don't want to push you into something you're not ready for."

"But I am ready, Daddy," she said. "I promise."

I studied her face, looking for any sign of reluctance. "Are you sure, little one?"

She nodded. "Yes, Daddy."

"If you feel uncomfy, you can stop me at any time, okay?"

She nodded and smiled. "I understand, Daddy."

I groaned and grabbed her waist. I flipped her over onto her back. I put my forearms on either side of her head. She looked up at me, biting her lip. Her eyes showed anticipation and excitement, but also trust. Fuck. I loved that she trusted me. I would do everything I could to make sure I didn't betray that trust.

I bent my head to capture her lips with my own. As I kissed her, I gently slid my hand up her thigh. She lifted her hips up to meet mine, making me groan in ecstasy.

9

Sophie

Ethan's lips felt absolutely amazing. And as his hand slid up my thigh, I felt my pussy grow wet. A shiver of excitement ran down me. I knew what was going to happen next.

Ethan's hand went to my underwear. He stroked it, feeling how wet it was. He groaned softly. "You're ready for this, aren't you little one?"

"Yes Daddy," I whispered. "Please. I want... I want you."

He kissed my forehead before resting his forehead against mine. "You have me, little one. You have me."

Slowly he peeled off my underwear and I lifted my hips up to let him. Once they were off, he pushed my skirt up to fully reveal my pussy. "You're so beautiful, little one," he said as he stroked my slit. "So beautiful."

I whined and moved my hips up and down. I wanted

him inside me more than anything. I felt so open and ready for him.

Ethan straightened up and unzipped his pants. He pulled out his huge, hard cock. I swallowed at the sight of it. How was that supposed to fit inside me?

He stroked it as he watched my reaction. "We can stop now if you prefer," he said gently.

"No," I said. "I want you. All of you."

Slowly he nodded and then placed the tip of his cock at my entrance. "I'll go slow," he said. "Just relax, little one. Daddy will take care of you."

He pushed inside me slowly. I whimpered as I felt myself stretch around him. But surprisingly it didn't hurt. I was already so wet and ready for him.

Ethan let out a shuddering groan. "Fuck, you feel so good, little one." He thrust into me. First he was slow until my body completely relaxed. Then he went faster and faster. I moaned and squeezed my eyes shut, getting lost in the sensations of having him inside me.

He reached down between us and started to play with my clit. I gasped as his finger touched it, sending a shock of pleasure through me. "Shh, just relax," he said. "I want you to come all over my cock, little one. But I need you to relax first."

I nodded. "Yes, Daddy."

"Good girl." He leaned down to trail kisses down my neck, his tongue snaking out to taste my skin as his fingers teased my clit. I felt pressure building inside my stomach, unlike any other sensation I had experienced.

Even though I had masturbated before and even

orgasmed, it didn't feel like this. This felt a million times better.

Finally the pressure became too much and I came. I became a shuddering mess as the pleasure tore through me. I gasped and shook underneath Ethan who was thrusting faster and faster inside of me, his breath dissolving into rapid pants.

Suddenly he stilled and he let out a shuddering gasp as he spilled his hot seed inside me.

For a second there wasn't any sound except the sounds of us catching our breath as we recovered from our orgasms.

Then Ethan rolled off of me and gathered me in his arms. "Are you okay, little one?" he asked. "Did that feel good?"

I nodded, smiling. I buried my face in his chest. "Yes, Daddy," I said. "That felt amazing."

"Good," he said, sounding relieved. "That felt amazing for me too." He stroked my hair as he held me. "You're such a good girl," he said. "I can't wait to spoil you and take care of you for as long as you let me."

I blushed and smiled happily. Ethan always made me feel so incredibly happy. "Maybe next time I could wear a diaper," I said.

"You want to?" He lifted his head to look at me, a soft smile on his face.

I nodded. "Hannah was wearing one earlier. It looked cute and comfy."

He smiled. "I think we can make that happen," he said. "You would look cute in a diaper." He stroked my hair. "It's time to go to bed, though. You have a big day of work ahead of you."

I nodded, thinking of all the orders I had now. "Yes, Daddy," I said, wrapping my arms around his waist. I closed my eyes, feeling completely and perfectly safe.

CARNAL BIKER DADDY

1

Ivy

It was nearly eleven at night and I struggled to keep my eyes open as much as I struggled to push away my irritation. I was home from college and my parents hadn't bothered to pick me up from the airport so I had to take a bus all the way back home and now I was walking home alone in the dark with my suitcase. In Newbury.

I hadn't expected them to drive me everywhere during my winter break. I knew how to get around all right on my own. But I hadn't seen them in three months and it was dangerous to walk around at night in Newbury. I had hoped they would at least pick me up tonight. But they hadn't even bothered to answer my texts or my phone calls.

"It's fine," I muttered as I lifted my suitcase over a large puddle on the sidewalk. "It's not like I haven't walked around Newbury before." I had grown up here, after all.

But this town was dangerous. The Demon biker gang was still alive and well, kidnapping women for their brothels and recruiting men for their drug mills. I had two former classmates from high school who had been captured by them. Only one of them had escaped alive. Another group had tried to drive them out awhile back, and had even scattered them for a little while, but the Demons were always around. They were basically rats. Impossible to get rid of.

I sighed and looked up at the night sky. At least it was gorgeous tonight with stars and the moon shining bright. I smiled. I had always loved looking at the night sky, even on cold nights like this one. It was so pretty.

Footsteps behind me startled me to alertness. I turned to see a man walking behind me. Terror gripped me and I started to walk faster. He picked up his pace as well. I turned a corner and so did he. That was never a good sign.

Then I started to run. I glanced behind me to see him running too. I shrieked and dropped my suitcase, trying to sprint faster. Maybe he would settle for my suitcase and leave me be.

But he was still following me. He was catching up to me. I could see him illuminated in the streetlight, a sneer on his face. The Demon insignia was plainly visible on his jacket.

I tripped on a rock and fell to the ground, scraping my hands and elbows. A scream escaped my lips. I struggled to my feet just as my kidnapper was inches away...

Just before he could reach me a motorcycle roared out of nowhere. It pulled up on the sidewalk between me and the man. The biker's head was covered in a helmet so I couldn't see him at all, but it was clear his attention was focused on the man. He pulled a gun out and pointed it at the man. I flinched, expecting a gunshot.

But there wasn't any. I heard running footsteps and knew my would-be kidnapper was running away. I should run too. But I was rooted to the spot. I was so close, this stranger could reach out and grab me if he wanted to and there wouldn't be anything I could do about it.

Finally, the biker put the gun away and turned to me. It was only then I managed to back up a couple of steps. *What the hell are you doing? Run!* But it wouldn't have mattered if I ran or not. He would find me. The biker inclined his head, as if he was looking me up and down. "Are you okay?" he asked.

I nodded numbly. I looked him over, looking for any sort of insignia on his clothes, wondering if I had just been kidnapped by another Demon biker, maybe one who outranked the one on foot. Or he was from the rival gang. I didn't know much about them because I was already going to college out of state when they moved into town. For all I knew, they were just as bad as the Demons. I tried to take another step back and stumbled back instead. Why couldn't my legs work properly?

"No, don't run. It's okay. I'm not here to hurt you." He took off his helmet, revealing a handsome face underneath. He looked older, possibly forty years old, but he was sexy. His dark hair was streaked with gray at the sides and laugh lines were visible on the corners of his eyes, making him look almost friendly. "My name is Hector. I'm with the Hell's Renegades."

Hell's Renegades. That must be the group that tried to chase out the Demons. At least he wasn't going to throw me into a brothel or drug deal like the Demons would. But I didn't know anything about the Hell's Renegades. For all I knew, they were worse. I slowly shook my head. "Ivy," I said. "My name is Ivy, but I-I don't know you. I need to go. My parents are waiting for me."

"Let me take you back to your place," he said. "I can escort you and keep you safe."

"I'll be fine."

He frowned slightly and an intimidating look entered his eyes. "You almost weren't fine," he said. "It's late at night and you're alone. It's dangerous."

I knew he was right and I knew he wasn't going to let me go. I looked down the sidewalk, wondering if I could make a run for it. He revved the motorcycle in response. "You can't outrun me," He said. "And I'm not going to let you go, not when you're alone. Let me take you home."

I nodded.

He handed me his motorcycle helmet. "Put this on. What's your address?"

I told him my address as I got on the motorcycle behind him. Tentatively, I wrapped my arms around his waist, blushing when I felt hard muscles beneath his jacket. *This is a mistake. Why the heck am I going with an absolute stranger?* But at the same time, there wasn't anything else I could do. We roared off down the street.

2

Hector

I slowed down when I reached her street so I could look out for her house number. She relaxed when we pulled onto her street. Maybe she finally realized I wasn't about to kidnap her or hurt her myself. Good. I hated it when women thought I was a monster. Unfortunately in this town, most of them did. Not to mention how they acted when me and the Hell's Renegade motorcycle club raided their brothels to rescue them. The fear in their eyes...

No. I couldn't think about that right now. I needed to focus on getting Ivy home safe.

It had been pure luck I saw her when I was leaving the club bar. I could tell she was in trouble by the way she was running but I managed to put myself between her and the idiot trying to kidnap her. I didn't blame her for not trusting me. Newbury was a dangerous town, after all. But

I wasn't about to leave her alone in the streets only to get kidnapped when I was out of reach.

When we reached her house, I parked in front of it. It looked dark, without even an outside light on. My suspicions were immediately raised. "Were they expecting you?" I asked.

"They should have been," she said. "I've been emailing them my travel plans. I texted them when I got off the plane." She bit her lip. "But they never responded. I guess it's been close to a month since I've actually talked to them."

I had a bad feeling about this. What sort of parent never responded to their child? Who the hell let their kid travel alone in Newbury late at night? That was asking for trouble. I went with her up to the window. I knocked on the door. No answer. Ivy reached into her pocket and pulled out a house key. She tried it in the door. It didn't work. "They changed the locks," she said. Her chin trembled slightly.

I peered inside one of the windows. "I don't see any furniture," I said. "Do your parents usually keep such an empty home?"

"No." Her arms crossed in front of her and her eyes went wide. "They couldn't have just moved, could they? We weren't close, but they knew I didn't have anywhere else to live. They would tell me if they were going somewhere else… wouldn't they?"

I wanted to put my arms around her and hug her tight. I couldn't even begin to imagine what she was feeling or going through. She had been abandoned by her parents in a dangerous town and she was with a perfect stranger that she had good reason not to trust. But I knew better than to try to hug her. She would just flinch away, not that I blamed her.

I looked at my watch. It was nearly midnight. "I'm sure there's a reason for this," I said. "But we need to get you somewhere safe tonight. I can take you to a hotel or something."

She shook her head. "No," she said, her voice breaking. "I'm not going anywhere with you! I want to be back with my family! I don't understand!" She covered her mouth with her hands and started to cry.

I clenched my hands into fists to keep myself from hugging her. "Look," I said. "If you don't want to go anywhere, you don't have to. You can stay here."

"They changed the locks and no one's home!"

I reached into my jacket pocket and pulled out a small lock-picking kit. I hadn't used this on private property in years. Ever since joining with the Hell's Renegades, I only picked locks to break people out of the Demon's compounds. But I would happily pick the locks to make sure Ivy was safe for the night. An empty house wasn't ideal, but I wasn't going to leave her outside on her porch all night. I wanted to make sure she was at least behind locked doors before I went home for the night.

It was a cheap lock and it was easy to pick. Too easy. Anyone with a YouTube tutorial and a bobby pin could pick this lock. Once I opened it up, I opened the door for her. She stared at me, looking like she couldn't tell if she should be horrified by me or grateful. "It's all right," I said. "Let's go in."

She went in first and I followed her. Just like I thought from the window, there was no furniture. No paintings or pictures on the walls. Not even an abandoned chair in the living room. In the kitchen, on the counter, was a "For Sale" sign waiting to be put up out front. It looks like this place was almost ready for market.

Ivy ran up the stairs to her room. I followed her upstairs, slowly. She was sitting in the doorway of one of the bedrooms, crying. "My room is empty," she said when I came upstairs. "Everything's gone. Everything I have is gone." She looked up, eyes wide. "My suitcase. I dropped my suitcase when I was running. That was everything I had."

I nodded. "Stay here. I'll find your suitcase and bring it back."

She bit her lip and then nodded. "Thank you," she said. "I'm so sorry to pull you into my mess."

I shook my head. "Don't apologize. I'm happy I found you so you wouldn't have to deal with this alone." I looked at her bedroom door, satisfied it had a lock on it. "Do me a favor and lock yourself in your bedroom until I come back. Don't leave this room."

She frowned. "Why?"

"Because when the realtor changed the locks, they put in a really cheap lock. If I could break into it easily, then so could the Demons. At least this way you'll have two cheap locks between you and danger instead of one."

She shivered. "Right."

I left her room and went to go find the suitcase.

3

Ivy

I sat on my bedroom floor, staring around the empty room. I had finished crying and now I felt numb. Everything was wrong. This entire night just felt like a huge nightmare.

My parents had never been sentimental or affectionate. They made sure I went to school on time and drove me to extracurriculars, but that was it. They never stayed to watch me during my dance recitals or cheer me on during my soccer games like the other parents did. I told myself I was okay with that.

When I moved to college, I was told anything I couldn't fit into my dorm room was going to get either sold or tossed out and my room turned mostly into a regular guest bedroom. But they still welcomed me home during my school breaks and didn't protest when I slept in the same room.

So I never thought they would just up and move without telling me. But there was no other possibility.

I don't know how long I stayed in that room, staring at the wall. Everything just became a blur. There was a knock on the bedroom door which made me jump. "It's me," Hector said on the other side.

Right. The big, scary biker that somehow was becoming more comforting than threatening. "Come in," I said. "I'm sure you can pick that lock too."

He opened the door and revealed my suitcase. "I'm guessing this is yours," he said. "Unless another person with a suitcase got chased down tonight."

I nodded. "Yes, that's mine. Thank you."

He handed it to me. "I don't suppose you have a sleeping bag in there do you?"

I snorted and shook my head.

"Then please let me take you to a motel," he said. "It's not safe in here and it won't be comfortable." A muscle in his jaw twitched. "I understand if you're scared of going to a motel with me, but I won't even enter the room if you don't want. Or you could call a friend and have them take you."

"I don't really have any friends in town," I said. "At least, not any friends I could wake up at midnight. I haven't even talked to most of them since high school." I sighed. "I guess a motel would be for the best."

He nodded. "Thank you," he said. "I would feel better if you slept in a bed tonight. And then we can figure it out in the morning. My motorcycle club can help you as well."

I frowned. "Why are you helping me?" I asked. "I don't understand. What do you get out of it?"

"The pleasure in knowing I won't see you in a Demon brothel the next time my club raids them," he said.

I winced. "Fair enough." I knew that was too real of a possibility.

He helped me to my feet and picked up my suitcase. "There's a motel only about ten minutes away," he said. "It's not fancy, but the locks on the doors are at least decent, so you'll be safe."

"Do I want to know why you know so much about locks?"

He smiled sheepishly. "I was an idiot when I was younger," he said. "I broke into people's homes and stole TVs, laptops, and anything else that would sell. I needed the money to support myself and I couldn't find any legitimate job that paid as well as stealing."

"What happened?"

"I broke into the wrong person's house and he caught me. He was president of the Hell's Renegades at the time and instead of calling the cops or beating the shit out of me, he took me in and welcomed me into the club. It set me straight."

I raised an eyebrow. "But you still carry around a set of lockpicks?"

He shrugged. "They come in handy."

We went back outside and got back on the bike. He managed to carry the suitcase even as he biked down the street.

It wasn't long before we pulled up to a nearby motel. It

was definitely sketchy looking. It features rooms with broken shades and overgrown shrubs. There was a single vending machine near the entrance with an "Out of Order" sign on it. The motel sign flickered, making me cringe a little. "Are you sure this place is safe?" I asked.

"It's the safest place I can take you." He raised an eyebrow at me. "Unless you want to go back to my place."

I shook my head. "No, thank you. No offense."

"None taken. It's smart not to trust anyone in this town. Especially bikers."

I snorted. "And yet I still have to trust you, don't I?"

"You don't have to trust me. You just have to do what I say. Understand?" He gave me a stern look that made me blush. It also sent a shiver down my spine that I didn't want to think about.

"Yes, sir," I said.

He winced and looked away. "You don't have to call me sir."

He checked me into the motel and walked me to my room. Outside the door, he handed me my suitcase. "Do you mind if I come back tomorrow?" he asked. "Just to see how you're doing?"

I should say no. I didn't know him after all and this felt like it was asking for trouble. But I found myself nodding. It was nice knowing there was someone looking out for me right now. Or at least someone who I could talk to about this.

He looked relieved. "Have a good night, Ivy," he said. "It's going to be okay. We'll sort this out in the morning."

I hoped he was right.

4

Hector

I came back the next day first thing in the morning. I picked up breakfast on the way, knowing she would probably be hungry.

I rocked up to the motel and got out to knock on her door. She answered it almost immediately. She gave me a weak smile but her face was tearstained. I wouldn't be surprised if she woke up crying.

My heart ached at the thought. Nobody deserved to be abandoned like she was. I wanted to make her feel better. And I was lying if I didn't admit I was attracted to her. She was absolutely beautiful.

Even now, dressed in a tank top and cotton shorts, I couldn't help but admire her sweet little curves. Her hair was parted into two pigtails as well, which made her look like a Little. Everything about her set off my Daddy instincts. I had to be careful with that. I accidentally used my Daddy voice with her last night. Her reaction had been beautiful. She immediately got submissive and blushed so cutely. But she had called me sir. All of the women trapped in Demon brothels were trained to call men sir. And after rescuing dozens of them and watching them tremble and flinch before me and stammer out, "I'm sorry, sir", the word made me sick.

I held out the takeout bag. "I thought you might want breakfast," I said.

She nodded. "Thank you. I appreciate it." She took the bag and pulled out a breakfast sandwich. She smiled and groaned as she ate it. "I forgot how hungry I was," she said. "But I had been traveling most of the day yesterday and I didn't get a chance to eat."

She had probably expected to eat when she got home.

With Ivy sitting down on her bed, I sat down in a nearby armchair, watching her eat. She visibly relaxed the more she ate which made me happy.

When she was done, she wiped her mouth. "I texted my mom but I haven't gotten a response. I'm going to call her today. But it's not so bad. I have some money saved up and this motel isn't horrible. I can always stay here for my winter break."

"That sounds depressing," I said. "We'll help you find your parents. I promise."

She frowned. "I don't see how a motorcycle club can help me find my parents."

I smiled slightly. "We can be surprising. If you want, I can take you to the Celtic Knot later and you can meet the other club members. Our chef, Blaine, makes some pretty decent food as well."

She smiled. "Thank you."

"It's no trouble at all. Trust me."

I stayed with her as she tried to call her mom but there was no response. I hated the fear and disappointment that flickered on her face when she couldn't make a connection. She had to be so scared out here alone, especially with a stranger like me.

I wanted to make her feel safe and comfy. I wanted to make her smile. But I wasn't sure the best way I could do that.

I stayed in the room while she got dressed in the bathroom. I was a little sad to see her out of the shorts and tank top and into practical winter wear. She had looked so cute in those clothes.

This isn't about you, asshole! Besides, would you rather she freezed?

I was being ridiculous. I couldn't keep thinking this way or I was no better than a Demon.

"Let's go to the Celtic Knot," I said. "I'll talk to Chase, my club president. He might have some ideas on how to find them. At the very least, you can get some decent food and coffee. I have a feeling that breakfast sandwich didn't do a lot to fill you up."

She nodded, crossing her arms in front of her. "That sounds good."

I took her to the Celtic Knot. She raised an eyebrow when we pulled into the Newbury Mall parking lot. "I didn't know this place was still open."

"Barely," I said, smiling. "But we try to bring some more life into it." Not only did we have the Celtic Knot, an Irish pub, and also our main hangout and headquarters, but we funded businesses to rent space in the the mall.

I led her inside. It was still early, so there was only Blaine at the bar. He looked up when we entered. "Hey Hector," he said. "What are you doing back here so early?" He looked at Ivy with a raised eyebrow. "Did you find an old lady?"

Ivy looked confused and I rolled my eyes at him. "Don't be an idiot. However, two coffees and Irish stew would be appreciated."

He nodded. "Coming right up."

"Is Chase around?"

"He's in the back. He's taking advantage of having the office to himself while Ethan is visiting Sophie."

Ethan managed a loan program to help Newbury residents create new businesses as an effort to revive the town after the Demons ripped it apart. He used to work from home, but then a Demon broke into his home and stole the loan information which put Sophie, the first loan holder, at risk. Now he shared Chase's office to keep the information more secure.

"Have a seat," I told Ivy. "I'll go talk to Chase."

She sat down at the bar, looking a little nervous. Hopefully after a little while, she would feel more comfortable.

Chase was in the back room, going over paperwork. He looked up at me. Like usual, he looked exhausted. There was a fading bruise over one of his eyes from the last time he had an altercation with the Demons. "Hey, Hector," he said. "What are you doing here?"

"I have a bit of a situation." I told him everything about Ivy and what happened last night.

Chase grimaced. "I can't even imagine letting anyone walk around Newbury in the middle of the night, let alone leaving them without a home." He ran his hand through his hair, thinking. "I have some connections with the realtors in the area. They might be able to give me some information on where her parents went if she can't reach out to them at all. Do you think you could take her in until then?"

"I don't think she would want to go back with me," I said. "She's with me because she doesn't have much of a choice. But she doesn't trust me either, not that I blame her."

"She trusts you enough to follow you to a motorcycle club bar. It couldn't hurt to ask."

5

Ivy

I was a little nervous being alone in the bar when Hector left. Sure I didn't know him that well, but I knew him better than Blaine.

But Blaine was nice too. He gave me some Irish stew and some coffee. It was delicious. "So what got you mixed up with the likes of Hector?" he asked. He had a nice Irish lilt that was fun to listen to.

"He saved me last night," I said. "I almost got kidnapped by a Demon, but luckily he was in the area." I shivered a little as I remembered how close I had been to danger. I probably owed Hector my life. I looked up at Blaine, a thought occurring to me. "Why did you call me an old lady?" I was only twenty-one. I didn't look old.

He smiled sheepishly. "I was just giving Hector shit," he said. "Don't worry about it."

"But what does it mean?"

Hector came up behind me. "It's club slang," he said. I jumped a little at the sound of his voice. I didn't realize how close he was. I looked at him but his face was unreadable. "It means significant other."

I blushed at the thought of that. I had to admit I didn't hate the idea. Hector was sexy and so far he had been more than kind to me. I wasn't used to having someone take care of me, but he seemed to do it as if it was natural.

He seemed to be pretty pissed at the thought, though. I didn't blame him. Why would he want someone like me? He probably thought I was just some silly kid.

"I was just messing with him," Blaine said as Hector sat down at the bar beside me. "He swears he'll never take an old lady. Something about feeling like a monster or bollocks like that."

Hector took a sip of the coffee Blaine gave him. "If you keep this up, I'll have to tell your old lady that you secretly like mac and cheese from a box despite being the club's culinary genius."

Blaine grinned. "As if she would believe you."

He went back to the kitchen, leaving Hector and me by ourselves. "What did the president say?" I asked.

"Chase knows some of the realtors in town and he's going to ask around about your house and your family. For the meantime, you can stay with me. My house isn't a lot, but it's more comfortable than a motel room."

I bit my lip.

He sensed my hesitation and looked away. "If you feel more comfortable staying with a club member who has an old lady, I understand. You could go with Chase or Blaine instead."

"No," I said quickly. "I-I would rather go with you. I know you a little better, after all. I just don't want to put you out. You've already done so much for me."

His brow furrowed. "I haven't done anything, not really."

"You saved me last night and you're trying to help me find my parents this morning. That's a lot for a near perfect stranger. I just don't understand why you're doing this."

"Because I want to." He smiled at me. "Really. I want to help."

I wasn't used to this. I wasn't used to someone helping. But it felt good. It felt good knowing I wasn't alone.

6

Hector

I could have killed Blaine for saying that shit about me and old ladies in front of Ivy. I didn't want to make her uncomfortable. But she didn't seem uncomfortable around me anymore. When we got on the bike to go back to the motel to get her stuff, she hugged my waist tighter and leaned her head against my back. Her small, curvy body felt good pressed up against me, as much as I didn't want to think about it. And after a good night's sleep and some good food, she seemed more relaxed, which I was happy about.

After picking up her things, we went back to my place. It was a small, slightly rundown house on the edge of town. I was able to get it for next to nothing because nobody was moving to Newbury these days, but I still hadn't gotten around to fixing it up. But at least I had a guest room and the locks worked on all the doors.

I took Ivy to the guest room. It was a little bland, with only a bed and nightstand in the room. But the bed was covered in a clean comforter and fluffy pillows. "This is yours," I told her. "There's also a good lock on the door if it makes you more comfortable."

She set down her suitcase. "Thank you," she said.

I nodded. "No problem. My room's down the hall. You can hang out in the kitchen or living room, or do anything you want, really." I turned to leave.

"Hey, Hector?"

I looked back at her. She was biting her lip hesitantly and I knew she was debating on what she was going to say. "Blaine said something about you thinking you're a monster. And I want you to know that you're not a monster."

That was sweet of her to say. "You don't even know me," I said. "For all you know, I'm not even helping you. I'm just trying to kidnap you, just like the Demons."

"I highly doubt that," she said, smirking. "Why are you so insistent on believing you're a monster?"

I sighed. "I don't think I'm a monster. It's more complicated than that. I live a dangerous life being part of the Hell's Renegades. We've been lucky so far in getting away from the Demons, but eventually that luck will run out. If I take an old lady, she'll end up getting hurt. They might even take her for their brothels. And I can't bear the thought of someone I love ending up there."

"But that sounds lonely for you," she said. "You shouldn't have to be alone."

"It's better than the alternative." I looked down. I

didn't know why she cared so much. She probably just saw me as some sad old man. But it didn't matter. I wasn't going to take an old lady. And I definitely couldn't take her. Just the thought of the Demons laying their hands on her made me sick to my stomach. "You should keep trying your parents," I said. "They might pick up this time around."

I left before could continue my train of thought. I didn't want to admit how much I was attracted to her and how I much I wanted to be her Daddy.

Instead, I decided to focus on what to make her for dinner. I wanted to make her a home cooked meal. I decided on baked chicken, mashed potato, and green beans.

I was peeling the potatoes when she came out a little later. "They're still not picking up," she said. "Is there anything I can do to help to cook?"

"Not at all, I want you to relax while I cook. Can you do that for me?"

She blushed and looked down. "Yes, s–... yes."

I realized I had used my Daddy voice on her again. I didn't even think about it. It just felt natural to do with her. And she responded so beautifully every time I did it, too. But I needed to be careful. I couldn't get attached to her or think about her that way.

"Why don't you watch a movie or something while I cook?" I asked. "It could be nice for you to properly relax. It's your winter break, after all."

She smiled. "Thanks. That's a good idea."

I watched as she went to the living room and turned

on the TV. I couldn't help but smile as she curled up on the couch. She looked so adorable and relaxed. It was too weak to imagine her cuddling with a stuffy, watching TV, feeling safe and protected. I wanted her to feel safe with me. I wanted to protect her...

No. I had to stop thinking about that. I didn't have a right to think about her like a Little. Besides, she would never want someone like me.

7

Ivy

Hector served me food on the couch, which was nice. I was never allowed to eat much in the living room because it would get dirty too fast. My parents told me I was only allowed to eat in the kitchen or in my room.

They encouraged me to spend as much time in my room as possible. While most of my classmates were forced to watch TV or spend time on the internet only in the living room, my parents gave me my own TV, computer, and video game consoles. But I had to keep them all in my room. It was years before I realized they did this on purpose to keep me out of the way. If I wanted to watch a tv show, I had to do it in my room. Play a game? I had to go to my room. Read a book? I had books in my room, didn't I? It was a way to keep me out of sight, out of mind. Eventually I was spending more time in my room than anywhere else in the house.

So it was surreal eating a homecooked meal in the living room, but it felt nice.

When Hector sat down with his own meal, I turned off my movie and handed him the remote. "Here you go," I said.

He raised an eyebrow. "What's this for?"

"So you can put on something you want to watch." I took a bite of the chicken and almost groaned. It tasted amazing.

Hector smiled softly and handed me back the remote. "Go back to what you were watching. You didn't have to stop because of me."

I frowned. "But I was halfway through the movie. And you would probably hate it anyway. It was a kids movie."

"I'm sure I'll love it," he said. "Come on, let's put it on."

I blushed, knowing what he was going to find. It was an off-brand kids movie I stumbled across when I was younger but I loved it. It was a retelling of Snow White, but instead of the Huntsman letting her go and her running off to live with seven dwarves, he takes her back to his place and they fall in love while battling the evil queen. It was a silly movie, but I enjoyed it.

We watched it together. I couldn't tell what he was thinking as we watched a scene with him dancing with her in the forest. He must be bored out of his mind watching this. But he didn't complain or seem to mind.

When the credits rolled, I turned to him, feeling a little anxious. "What did you think?" I asked.

He stood up to take our dishes into the kitchen. "I think he should have let her go," he said. "It wasn't right to trap her in his house like that. There had to be another way."

"But he was protecting her," I said. I got up to follow him into the kitchen. "The evil queen was looking for her and she would have killed them both if she found them."

Hector started to wash the dishes. "He could have found another way. He did it because he was attracted to her. He was using her from the start."

"He wasn't using her. She was in love with him."

"She didn't know any better. She had been imprisoned her whole life and had never known any sort of protection before so of course she fell in love with the first person who gave a shit about whether she lived or died. He should have known better. He had all the power, was older–"

"They were the same age."

Hector looked surprised and then he looked away. "Must have missed that part."

I took a step closer to him. "You're not really thinking about the movie, are you?"

He gave a half smile. "Of course I am. What else would I be thinking about?"

My heart was pounding with anxiety. I knew what I wanted to ask but how would he react? What if he insisted on me moving in with one of his club members instead of staying with him? I had already pushed him a lot and he barely knew me. Why would he open up to me about this? "You've been fighting the Demons for years now, haven't you?"

He looked a little surprised at the change of topic. "Yes," he said.

"You've saved a lot of women from them, haven't you?"

A muscle twitched in his jaw. "I have."

"Is that why you feel like the Huntsman?"

I waited for him to tell me I was way off base and that it wasn't any of my business. But instead he sighed and ran his fingers through his hair. "I hated it every time I rescued people," he confessed. "But because I'm the best at picking locks, I was always the one who opened the door. Sure, most of them are usually... working when we arrive and the other club members take care of them. But there are ones who were just kidnapped or who were too sick or bruised to work. I would be in charge of getting them to safety. And I got to see them every time in wretched conditions, usually beat to shit. Most of them were terrified of me." He grimaced. "But now and then, a woman would be grateful. And she would try to show her gratitude the way the Demons had trained her. And I would feel like a monster every time it happens."

"Saving people doesn't make you a monster."

"No. But I'm a monster because I wanted it." His lip curled. "I wanted them to take care of and protect but I also wanted them in my bed. I knew they were only doing it because they were scared and grateful but it didn't stop me from being tempted." He turned away and leaned against the counter with his back facing me. "I told you earlier I didn't want an old lady because I didn't want the Demons hurt. But I'm also worried I would end up hurting her myself."

Before I could think better about it, I came up behind him and wrapped my arms around his waist. "I don't think you're capable of hurting someone you care about," I said, leaning my forehead against his back. "Besides, you saved my life without even thinking about it. No monster would do that."

He snorted. "I just did what anyone would do."

"Not many people would themselves between a Demon and a perfect stranger," I said. "And you didn't even ask for anything in return."

He turned around slowly, but I kept my arms around me. Emotions warred in his eyes. I couldn't tell what he was thinking. I didn't know if I could dare think it. "You should be careful around me," he growled. "I'm not some prince charming. You're right, I didn't ask for anything. But that doesn't mean I don't want it."

I blushed and felt a shiver run down my spine even as I felt my pussy grow wet at his words. "What if I want you too?"

He shook his head slowly. "You don't want an old man like me. Not really."

"You can't tell me what I want and what I don't want," I said. "I want you."

8

Hector

Ivy stared up at me, looking earnest. I wanted her so badly. I wanted to believe her. Could she really mean it? Could she really want me? I was easily twice her age. But I had told her my dirty little secret and she hadn't backed away. There wasn't a flicker of fear or hesitation.

I could scarcely dare to believe it.

Slowly I lowered my face to hers and pressed my lips against hers. Ivy sighed and kissed me back eagerly. I groaned and wrapped my arms around her body. It felt so sweet holding her like this while kissing her.

Her hips brushed up against mine and my cock grew hard. I knew she felt it but she didn't shy away.

I put my hands onto her hips and lifted her up onto the counter. "You're so beautiful," I growled. "I have no right to want you, but I do. I want you to be mine, baby girl."

"I'm yours," she whispered. "I'm all yours."

I trailed kisses down her neck, listening to her breath hitch with every kiss. I would never get used to those noises from her. They sounded like the sweetest music possible. "Stop me when you need to," I said as I slowly lowered the straps of her tank top.

In response she leaned back, giving me better access to her chest. "Keep going," she said breathlessly.

I trailed kisses down to her breast as I slowly peeled her shirt down and then her bra. Her perky little nipple sprang free and I claimed it with my mouth as my hand went to tease her other one. She whimpered and started to squirm as her breath started coming in soft pants. I knew if I slipped a hand into her pants then I would find her pussy soaked with need.

Her own hand traveled down to the waistband of my pants. I shut my eyes as she slipped her hand into my pants and squeezed around my cock. "Fuck," I muttered. "You feel so fucking good."

She stroked my cock in my pants until I couldn't take it anymore. I unbuttoned her pants and slid them off her before unbuttoning my own pants. My hand went to her pussy and just like I thought, she was wet, really wet. I slid my cock inside her and she gasped. I buried my face in her neck. She felt so fucking amazing.

Ivy gasped. "Fuck, Hector," she whispered.

"Call me, Daddy, baby girl," I growled. "I'm your Daddy, understand?"

She shivered. "Yes, Daddy," she whimpered.

As I thrust into her over and over I reached down to

play with her clit as I nipped at her neck with my teeth. Her entire body started shaking and she came all over my cock. That was enough to send me over the edge and I came inside her. I let out a shuddering breath as we held each other.

For a moment, neither or us moved and spoke. And then I slowly pulled out of her. She whimpered as I did so. I wrapped my arms around her shoulders and held her tight to me. She buried her face in my chest. "Are you okay, baby girl?" I asked.

She nodded. "Yes, Daddy," she said. "That felt so good."

I started to breathe again, feeling relieved. I had gone quick and rough. I was worried I had hurt her. "I love hearing you call me that," I confessed.

She pressed a kiss against my neck. "It feels right," she said. "I feel like you'll protect me and take care of me." She frowned. "I've never called any man that, not even my own father. But with you, it feels right."

"I will take care of you and protect you," I said, stroking her hair. "I promise. For as long as you want me to."

She smiled. "Thank you, Daddy."

I hugged her closer to my chest. I would do everything in my power to make sure she was safe. I had to be careful not to hurt her. So far she seemed relaxed and happy with things. She didn't even seem to mind that I fucked her on my kitchen counter, even though she deserved so much more than that. She deserved tenderness and love, not hard and rough sex.

I picked her up and carried her to my bedroom. "I want you to sleep in my bed tonight," I said. "With me. Can you do that?"

"Yes, Daddy," she whispered. "Please."

I smiled. "Good girl."

"Can we cuddle first, Daddy?"

"Of course, baby girl. And if you have any questions at all, you can ask me, okay? I don't want you to feel scared to ask me."

She smiled. "Thank you, Daddy," she said.

I kissed the top of her head as I set her down in my bed. I would do everything in my power to make sure she was happy, that was for sure.

9

Ivy

I curled up against Hector under the blankets. He had taken off everything except his underwear. I trailed my hand over his chest, fascinated with his muscles. He was older but was still in great shape. "I'm surprised," I said. "I'm surprised you would want someone like me."

"Someone like you?" He raised an eyebrow at me.

"I'm practically a kid compared to you," I said. "Not to mention all I do is ask for favors from you, eat your food, sleep in your house..."

The corners of his mouth quirked up. "You? Ask for favors? Hardly, baby girl. You seem really concerned with troubling me even though it's a pleasure to have you around, even if you don't sleep with me."

I blushed and looked down. "I don't want to be a nuisance," I said. "But that's all I seem to be."

"Is that how your parents made you feel?" He asked.

I bit my lip. It was the truth, whether or not I wanted to admit it. "They really weren't bad," I said. "They made sure I was fed and clothed and got to school on time. They never forgot my birthday and they helped me with things like getting my drivers' license and applying to colleges. But they always seemed a little annoyed about having a kid. More than anything, they wanted me out of the way, even though they never outright got that. Sure, they made sure I was safe, but I never got the feeling that they loved me."

"I'm sorry," he said. "You never should have gone through that."

"But it wasn't bad."

"You should have been loved, baby girl." He kissed my forehead. "I've already known you a short time and I know how sweet and lovable you are. And the fact that you didn't get that from your own parents is awful." He ran his fingers through my hair. I loved that feeling. It felt so good. "You know you don't owe me anything, right?"

I looked up at him. "I owe you everything."

He shook his head. "No. You don't owe me anything at all. I helped you because it pleased me to do so, understand? I don't want you sleeping with me if you're doing it out of obligation."

I smiled and snuggled up even closer to him. "Trust me," I said, wrapping an arm around his waist. "I'm sleeping with you because I was to. You're so sexy."

He chuckled. "I'm twice your age, baby girl. How you can find me sexy is beyond me."

"But I do." I closed my eyes, feeling my entire body

relaxed. "When I'm with you, I feel safe and beautiful. You're everything I ever wanted in a man. I don't care if you're a little older than me."

He kissed my forehead. "I'm glad, baby girl. Let's get some sleep, all right? I don't want you too sleepy in the morning."

"Yes, Daddy," I said.

He smiled. "Good girl."

The way he said it made a pleasant shiver run down my spine.

The next morning, I woke up to my phone ringing. I looked over to see Hector still asleep. I got out of bed and ran out of the room with my phone. I looked at the caller ID. It was mom. I answered it, feeling relieved. "Mom? Are you okay?"

"Yes, Ivy, of course we're okay," she said. She sounded impatient. "But why did our realtor call us, telling us some biker gang is looking for us?"

"Motorcycle club," I said. "They're my friends. You weren't picking up so I asked them to find you."

"Well, we didn't need to be found, especially by them," she said. "We moved out of Newbury a month ago to get away from all the bikers."

"Why didn't you tell me?" I felt a little sick. I wanted her to ask how I was or even if I was safe. But I knew that wasn't going to happen. "I walked home at night alone. I almost got kidnapped and I just found an empty house."

"You should know better than to walk around Newbury at night," Mom said. "I'm sure we told you we moved and you just forgot."

"No," I said. "You didn't."

"Well, it doesn't matter anyway. It's not like you had any stuff left at the house and you're away at college most of the time anyway. Not to mention you're twenty-one years old. You're more than capable of finding a place to stay for winter break."

I sat down on the floor in the hallway, feeling suddenly exhausted. "Can I ask you something, Mom?"

She sighed. "If you make it quick."

"Do you even want to see me again?" I didn't bother asking if she loved me. I wasn't ready to hear the answer on that.

She was silent for a second. "Look," she said, her voice softer. "I know it's hard growing up and leaving the nest, but it's important you grow a little more independent. I'm sorry I'm not the type of mother to faun all over her kids as if they're the most important thing in the world. But you are a perfectly pleasant person to spend time with. Maybe over the summer, we can grab dinner or something. But you can't stay with us. Our new house doesn't have a guest room."

That was the closest I would get to affection from Mom. I knew it was downhill from here. She was done with me. "Have a good day, Mom," I said. "I love you."

"Enjoy your break." She hung up without another word.

I put down my phone, feeling stunned. My stomach hurt.

"Was that your mom?" asked Hector.

I looked up at him. I hadn't even realized he was in the

doorway. I nodded. "They moved and didn't care to tell me. She didn't even apologize."

His jaw clenched for a second before he nodded and sat down on the floor next to me. "I'm sorry, baby girl," he said. He pulled me into his arms. "Do you want to talk about it?"

I buried my face into his chest. "There's nothing to talk about," I said. "She just doesn't want me. I don't think she would care if I even talked to her again."

His arms tightened around me. A tear slipped down my cheek. I didn't even realize I was on the verge of crying until that very moment. Hector brushed it away before I could react. "It's all right, baby girl," he said, rubbing my back. "Just let it all out."

We sat like that on the floor for several hours. I cried off and on until I felt exhausted. Hector kept rubbing my back and holding me. Now and then he would murmur reassurances to me. He didn't complain about being on the floor or about me getting heavy. He just let me process.

Finally, I spoke. "I think I'm better now," I said.

He kissed my forehead. "Are you sure? We can stay here a little longer."

I shook my head and started to stand up. I realized how stiff I was. I couldn't imagine how cramped Hector must have been being under me on the ground. He stood up and stretched, wincing. "Sit down at the table," he said. "I'll make us some breakfast."

Before we could move, his phone rang. He swore under his breath. "I'll be there in a second, little one."

I nodded and went to the kitchen table. I sat down,

crossing my legs under me in the chair. Even though I was sitting upright on a hard chair, I felt like I was going to fall asleep.

I could hear Hector's voice down the hall, but I couldn't make out what he was saying. When he approached me, his face was grim. "I have to go," he said. "There's an emergency at the club."

10

Hector

I hated leaving Ivy at home alone, especially after such a rough morning. Just the thought filled me with anxiety. I hadn't even had a chance to take her shopping for clothes and stuffies and anything else she might need to feel more comfy. But the club needed me.

I hugged her tightly to me. "Lock to door after I leave," I said. "And keep the shades drawn until I come back."

She nodded. "Yes, Daddy."

"Good girl." I kissed her. "Make sure you eat something and try to relax. I'll try to get back to you as soon as possible."

She buried her face in my chest. "Stay safe, Daddy. Please."

"I'll do my best, baby girl."

I left the house, looking back one last time before I

went to my bike and sped off down the road to the Celtic Knot.

I didn't want her to worry about the details so I had been vague. But in reality, the emergency was much worse. One of the club presidents had been shot.

When I got to the Celtic Knot, all of the club members were there, including several old ladies. I looked around for chase, but he was nowhere to be found.

Ethan greeted me first. "Hey," he said. "He's in his office, getting updated."

"Is Mac okay?" I asked.

"We don't know anything." He looked grim. "He had to go to the hospital. Ginger is going with him now." Ginger was Mac's old lady.

"What happened?"

"Some idiot Demons tried kidnapping women from Mac's town again. He and his club retaliated and got the women out of there but he was shot on the way out."

I grimaced. It looked like some of our luck was starting to run out.

Everyone in the Celtic Knot was unusually silent. There was usually a lot of noise and laughter, sometimes a poker game as well. But now everyone was sitting, waiting impatiently for the news. Very few people had drinks in front of them, and for once Blaine wasn't serving. He was leaning against the bar, arms crossed.

After awhile, Chase came out of his office. "He'll live," he said. "The bastard got him in the shoulder, but he'll be okay as long as Ginger can convince him to take it easy for a couple of months."

There was a collective sigh of relief. People slowly started talking again. The pit in my stomach started to unclench a little, but I knew it wouldn't last long. I needed to talk to Chase.

I made my way over to the club president. He was hugging his Little tight to him, as if he needed comfort from her more than anything. I had never seen him like this before and knew this affected him more than he was letting on.

Part of me didn't want to do this. I knew this was a bad time, but I knew I wouldn't change my mind. I didn't want to think about what would Ivy do if I came back shot or worse.

Chase looked at me and then let his old lady go. "Hector," he said. "You look like you want to talk."

"I do. If it's a bad time, it can wait until tomorrow."

"No, it's as good a time as any. I need a drink though. Why don't you join me at the bar?"

We went to the bar where Blaine was pouring everyone shots of whiskey to celebrate. He glanced at us both and gave us both a shot of whiskey as well. We downed them in one gulp.

Chase sighed, his shoulders relaxing marginally. "Hell of a day," he said. "And it's not even dark outside yet." He glanced at me. "Some of the club members are wanting to retaliate on Mac's behalf and I don't blame them. There's going to be a raid tonight. Are you coming?"

"That's the thing," I said. "I don't think I can do that anymore. No more raids. I can't keep taking risks like that."

He raised an eyebrow and then nodded. "Okay."

"Okay? You don't very surprised."

"I could tell how much it weighed on you every time we raided a Demon compound. Sure, it bothers all of us, but you really took it to heart. I knew it was only a matter of time before you couldn't take it anymore."

"Are you angry?"

He shook his head. "I can't blame you. It's tough and it's dangerous. Besides, you have an old lady to take care of now."

I frowned. "What the hell are you talking about?"

"Come on, Hector. Are you really going to try to tell me you're not with Ivy? I could hear how you talked about her yesterday and Blaine heard it too. It was obvious it was only a matter of time."

I sighed. "I didn't mean for it to happen," I said. "I don't want her to get hurt."

"You're the last person who would hurt someone intentionally," Chase said. "Especially someone you care about. I think you're in the clar."

"I hope so."

After knowing that Mac was safe and talking with Chase and some other club members more, I was ready to go back home to Ivy. It was agreed that I wouldn't go on any more raids with the club. I was still more than welcome at the Celtic Knot and I was still officially involved, but I wouldn't be putting my life at risk anymore. I was happy about that. I had more important things to handle.

On the way back home, I stopped at a store to grab a

teddy bear. I planned to get a lot more stuffies for Ivy but this would do for now.

When I came home, I found her in the living room, watching a movie. She stood up when she saw me. "Is everything okay?" she asked.

I nodded. "Everything is all right, little one," I said. "One of the club members got shot but he's going to be okay."

She blew out a sigh of relief. "That's so scary."

"It's okay. I'm not going to be going on any more raids so you don't have to worry about that. I promise."

She wrapped her arms around my waist. "Well, I'm glad about that."

"I also have something for you." I held up the teddy bear. "It's not much but we'll build up your collection of stuffies. Don't worry about that."

She grinned as she took the teddy bear and hugged it to her chest. "Thank you, Daddy!" she said. "I haven't had a stuffy since I was a kid."

I smiled. "I hope you like it."

"I love it."

I love you. I held the words back. Now wasn't the day to say it. That would come later. Right now I just wanted to spend as much time as I could with my Little.

11

Ivy

"Are you sure you want to do this, baby girl? You don't have to do it if it makes you uncomfortable."

"I'm sure, Daddy. Please. I want you to put a diaper on me."

He nodded and smiled as he held up the diaper. "Then get on your back, baby girl so I can put this on you."

I layed down on the bed.

"Lift your hips, baby girl."

I lifted my hips up and he slid the diaper underneath me.

He smiled. "Good girl. You can lower them now."

I relaxed my body and he put the diaper on me so it fit snugly but was comfy.

"How does that feel, baby girl?

"Amazing, Daddy," I said, sitting up.

It had been a year since I became Hector's Little and I never felt happier. I had just graduated college and was officially moved in with him full time. For the past year, I had learned a lot about being a Little and having a Daddy and the more I learned, the more I liked it. Today was the first time I was trying a diaper.

Right now, we were lying on the bed together. He wrapped an arm around me and pulled me close to him so our bodies were touching. "You look so cute with that diaper on," he said as he kissed my neck. "I just want to rip it off of you again."

I giggled. "Don't you dare! I like wearing it."

He grinned. "I'm glad you do, baby girl. I want you to be happy and comfy."

I always felt happy and comfy around him. And even better was that he was finally starting to believe it. After a year, he finally didn't think he was going to hurt me.

Hector kissed me as he got on top of me on the bed, pinning me down. He groaned as he kissed me and I felt myself get wet. But after only a few moments, he stood up, letting me go. "Come on," he said. "I want to take you somewhere, baby girl."

I frowned as I stood up. "Where are we going? The Celtic Knot?"

He shook his head. "Somewhere else. Away from people."

Intrigued, I followed him out of the house and to the bike. It wasn't often we went to someplace new. Unless he was visiting me at college, we didn't go many places except for the bar. There just weren't many places in Newbury.

Hector drove us out of town on his bike. It wasn't long before we crossed the town line and kept going until we reached a shimmering blue lake. He slowed down and stopped in front of the lake. "We're here, baby girl," he said.

I gasped softly as I looked out at the water. "It's beautiful," I said.

"I'm glad you like it. I wanted to take you someplace different. I know you must be feeling stir crazy now that you don't have college classes to keep you busy."

I giggled. "Maybe in a couple of months I'll be feeling stir crazy but not yet. However, this place looks gorgeous."

"I'm glad you like it. Let's walk on the beach for awhile." He grabbed my hand and we walked along the shore. The lake was devoid of people but it was far from silent. The water lapped up onto the shore and birds called in the distance. The wind blew through the air, cooling my skin. The sun was starting to set and the sky was beginning to glow a bright orange with the sunset.

"I feel like I could stay here forever," I said. "Can we buy a lakehouse, Daddy?"

He chuckled and kissed my forehead. "Maybe in a couple of years."

I pouted slightly, but I wasn't serious. I never expected him to say yes.

He cleared his throat. "Actually, there is something I want to ask you, Ivy. It might be a little soon. I understand if you want to wait, but I want to ask you anyway. If I'm being honest, I've wanted to ask you for about a year."

I frowned. "What are you talking about?"

He stopped walking suddenly and grabbed my hand. "You make me incredibly happy, Ivy," he said, laying his forehead against mine. "When I'm with you, I'm the happiest man alive."

I smiled, closing my eyes. "I'm definitely the luckiest Little alive with you, Daddy."

Hector smiled. "I'm glad you feel that way, baby girl." He brushed a piece of hair out of my face. "I want to spend the rest of my life with you. We can wait until you're ready but I've never been more sure of anything in my life." He reached into his pocket and pulled out a small velvet box. "Will you marry me, baby girl? Will you be mine?"

I couldn't stop the grin forming on my face even as I felt tears prick my eyes. Hector wanted to marry me?

I don't know why I was surprised, but I was. Sometimes I forgot how much he loved me even though he told me every day.

"Baby girl?" A trace of fear had entered Hector's voice and I realized I hadn't said anything for several seconds.

"Yes, I'll marry you," I said. "Oh my god, yes, Daddy. Of course I'll marry you."

He grinned, relieved. "Thank god. It would have been a long bike ride home if you said no." He slipped the ring on my finger and kissed me. "You're perfect," he said. "And I'm so happy you said yes." He kissed me again, this time longer. I wrapped my arms around him, enjoying the kiss. Once we broke off, he pressed his lips against my forehead. "I love you, baby girl."

I smiled and closed my eyes. "I love you too, Daddy." For once, everything felt right.

LOVING BIKER DADDY

1

Tina

I counted my tip money from an eight-hour shift of waiting tables while doing some mental math in my head. Once I added this money to the meager pile of savings from the rest of the tips this week, I should have just enough money to buy some groceries, which was good because my cupboards was more or less empty right now.

I left the restaurant where I worked to get into my car. I couldn't wait to sit down and take a break from my sore feet.

However, someone came up behind me when I reached my car. I felt someone grab my arm just as I grabbed my car door handle.

I turned around with a gasp. "What are you…"

My voice trailed off when I saw a man dressed in a leather jacket. He leered down at me, "Hey, Tina," he said.

My mouth went dry. "How do you know my name?"

"I'm... old friends with your father."

"I haven't spoken to him in years." He kicked me out when I was 15 and I hadn't seen him since.

"That's not my problem, now is it?" He grinned down at me. "But what is my problem is he's dead now. Did you know?"

I gritted my teeth as I tried to process this information. I should feel sad. But I mostly felt indifferent. I made peace long ago about never seeing my father again. "Like I said. I haven't spoken to him in years. I would like to leave now."

His grip on my arm got harder. "I don't think so, baby," he said. "Your father owes me a debt. And without him around to pay it, that falls to you."

"I don't have the money to pay it," I said.

He looked me up and down with a sly smile. "That won't be an issue, baby. With a sweet little body like yours, I can put you to work just fine."

My skin crawled. "How long do I have to get you the money?"

"I could just take you with me right now. No need to worry about the money."

The door to the diner opened and a laughing couple walked out. The man in front of me looked over at them and grimaced. "I guess I can be generous," he said. "I'll give you two days to get me thirty grand in cash. That's it. If you don't have it then I'll take you instead. And don't even think about running to the Hell's Renegades or the cops or some shit like that. I'll be watching you to make sure you behave."

My frazzled brain caught onto the phrase "Hell's Renegades". I had no idea who they were but I would have to find out. Because clearly this man thought they were a threat to him. So maybe they would be able to help me.

The man backed away, towards a motorcycle on the other side of the parking lot. I watched as he got on and sped away.

I forced myself to take deep breaths. I needed to be careful about this. Obviously I didn't have thirty grand and I didn't want to pay my father's debt anyway. Of course, it was just like him to find one more way to screw me over.

I went to the local library instead of going home. I needed to find out more about the Hell's Renegades, which required an internet connection. I longed to be snuggled up in my bed with my favorite stuffy, recovering from work to come back tomorrow, but that would have to wait. I managed to get on a library computer and looked up the Hell's Renegades. A bunch of articles came up at once about them. My throat went dry as I read through it. It looked like the local newspaper printed it every time the police expected the motorcycle club was involved in crimes. And there were a lot of them. Underground gambling, vandalism, and suspected kidnapping were the biggest ones, but nothing was ever pinned on them.

They definitely weren't people you would want to cross. And, according to the newspaper, they had a base of operations in town. It was a bar called Hawk's Landing.

I didn't want to reach out. They seemed like bad news and bars were exactly the places I steered clear from. But I remembered that man's threats of putting me to work. I needed help. And the Hell's Renegades were my best chance at it.

I took a deep breath and got into my car and drove to Hawk's Landing. Here goes nothing.

2

Talon

As I managed the bar at Hawk's Landing, I tried to fill a drink order while looking over a sales report at the same time and managed to spill beer all over a piece of paperwork. I swore as I grabbed a bar table to mop it up.

Laughter behind me made me glance back. Hawk, the former club president, was leaning against the bar, waiting for the beer on tap I managed to overfill. "Are you sure you don't want your old job back?" I asked as I handed him the beer.

"I'm good," He said. "I needed to retire. I want to spend as much time with Ramona as I can."

In all of the years I had known Hawk, he had always appeared invincible. He led the Hell's Renegades effortlessly, or at least that's what it looked like. His face was more lined now, his hair more gray. He was still strong and cut an imposing figure, but he was exhausted and ready to hand over the reins. He chose me to take over as club president. And I wasn't sure if I was up for the role, especially after a week of managing it. "How did you do this?" I asked. "Between running the poker tables, the bar, and fighting the Demon biker gang, how were you able to manage it all?"

"You get used to it after awhile." Hawk said. "Give it time. The men trust and respect you." He grinned. "But you might want to hire some help instead of trying to multitask like this."

I grimaced and knew he was right. Some help would be appreciated. Maybe Axel would like a break from debt collection to tend to the bar.

The door opened right then and I looked past the small crowd of bikers and people playing poker to see a woman in a waitress uniform come in. She looked terrified as she looked around, clutching her purse to herself. She was adorable with long dark hair pulled into a neat braid down her back. Her waitress uniform consisted of a short dress that showed her long, slender legs. I straightened up. "It looks like someone needs some directions." It was either that or they needed to call a tow truck. Women like her didn't come in here for pleasure unless they personally knew a biker in here. And I had never seen her around before.

Hawk glanced back at her, assessing the situation. "I wouldn't be too sure," he said. He downed his beer in one go. "I'm going to take a walk before I'm tempted to get involved in club business again. Good luck."

I raised an eyebrow as he left. He nodded at the

woman as he passed her. She shrank back away from him but managed a small smile.

I watched her as she approached the bar and sat down. "C-could I have a water, please?" she asked. Her eyes were fixed on the club insignia on my jacket.

"Sure," I said." I poured her a glass of water and watched her try to pick it up. Her hands were shaking so badly she poured water on the bar top. She quickly put the glass back down. "I'm sorry," she said.

"It's all right." I looked at her, trying to figure out what Hawk easily saw with just a glance. I could guess at it. "My name is Talon. I'm the president of the Hell's Renegades. Are you looking for someone?" I glanced at the poker tables and everyone playing. "Are you looking for a boyfriend or husband who lost track of time playing poker?"

She shook her head. "No. Um. I'm sorry. I shouldn't have come here." She moved to stand up.

"Wait," I said. "You clearly came here for a reason. I can help you. Just tell me."

The woman bit her lip. "I-I think I'm in trouble. My dad owed money to someone but I guess he died recently and they're coming after me to collect. I don't have the money."

"Who was this person?" I asked.

"He didn't give me his name. He just said he would be watching me and he told me not to contact the Hell's Renegades." She shrugged. "So I found out where you all hung out and I was hoping somehow you could help me." She shuddered. "I wouldn't be here if it wasn't important."

I believed that. She was so scared of me, she couldn't even look me in the eye. Whoever threatened her must have terrified her half to death. "Let's go in my office," I said. "It's quieter in there. You can tell me everything."

She looked around. "I'd be alone with you?"

I raised an eyebrow. "I'm not going to hurt you if that's what you're worried about."

"I would feel better..." Loud laughter from a nearby table drowned out her words.

"Listen," I said. "If I'm going to help you then I need to understand everything and that will probably be a long conversation which will go smoother if it's quiet. Not to mention if someone is watching you, then they will have seen you pull up here and if they're stupid, they could come in after you."

Her face went really pale.

"Don't worry," I said. "If they come in, they're dead. We don't throw people to the wolves here, especially when they ask for our help. But I doubt you want to witness a shootout."

She nodded rapidly. "I don't."

"Then follow me to the back office."

I signaled Axel and told him to man the bar before I went into the back office. She followed behind me. "I didn't catch your name," I said as I opened the office door for her.

"Oh right. My name is Tina."

I nodded and smiled at her. "It's nice to meet you, Tina."

The office looked exactly the same as when Hawk was

in charge. A desk and chair with very little decoration was on one side of the office while on the other was a leather couch. A small stuffy belonging to Hawk's old lady, Ramona, was on the couch. Tina stood in the doorway and stared at it, her face blank.

"Have a seat," I said.

That broke her out of her trance and she sat down on the couch. "Thanks," she said.

I sat down behind the desk. "Tell me more about the man who threatened you."

"Well, he was tall– I guess as tall as you. And he had dark hair and a motorcycle." She swallowed. "He told me if I couldn't get him the money in two days then he would put me to work. He said... he said I had a sweet little body." She looked at the stuffy again.

"Pick it up," I told her.

She looked at me, surprised. "Sorry?"

"I can tell you want to pick up the stuffy. So do it. It'll make you feel better." My tone came out harsher than I meant it to.

Tina flushed scarlet but she reached out and picked up the stuffy. She held it to her chest. My chest tightened at the sight. I wanted to reach out and comfort her. But I had to be professional and unattached. It would be the only way I could help her.

3

Tina

I hugged the teddy bear tight to me. I couldn't imagine why it would be in Talon's office in the first place. It felt out of place in a biker bar. But it made me feel better. Talon was looking at me, his face unreadable. I bit my lip. What was I even expecting him to do? Hunt down an annoying loan shark and kill him? I didn't even know the man's name. Not to mention I would never want anyone killed over me. I felt sick to my stomach just thinking about it.

"It sounds to me like your father owed money to the Demon biker gang. They deal in brothels and drugs."

The knot in my stomach tightened. It wouldn't surprise me if my father got addicted to drugs. When I was living with him, he spent most of his money on gambling and alcohol. I guess it got even worse with him. "He could have gotten involved with them," I said. "I haven't spoken to him in years. I don't know what he got into."

Talon's expression softened a little. "We can help you, Tina. You won't have to pay them, I promise."

"What are you going to do?" I asked.

"Well, he said you needed to pay him back in two days, right? I'll have some bikers tail you for protection until then. When he shows up, we'll make it clear you're protected. He'll back off when that's clear."

I bit my lip. I didn't like the idea of strangers tailing me for two days but it was better than the alternative. "Thank you," I said. "I-I don't have any money to give you. Is there any other way I can repay you?" I blushed when I realized what he might want. I had to admit Talon was gorgeous, but he scared the shit out of me. I doubted I would be able to sleep with him, even if it got me out of this mess. "I-I mean I can wait tables and clean and stuff. Maybe I could work off the deb that way."

He shook his head. "No. We don't charge for protection. You won't owe us anything."

It felt took good to be true. Would I really be out of this mess so easily? Just two days and it would be over? "Thank you."

He smiled. "No problem. I'll walk you out. And I'll have someone follow you to make sure you get home safely."

It was probably stupid to trust him. But I didn't know what else to do. Not unless I wanted to uproot my entire life. I did that once already. I didn't want to do it again.

Talon stood up with me and I was struck with how

much bigger he was than me. He was at least a foot taller than me and he was muscular. Even under the leather jacket I could tell he was built with muscle. His dark eyes matched his hair which was long, but didn't hide the jagged scar on his eyebrow. He was terrifying.

I realized we had been staring at each other for a second and I looked away. I was still holding the stuffy. My cheeks burned as I put it back down on the couch. He probably thought I was so childish.

"You can take it with you, if you want," he said.

I shook my head. "No. Thank you." As if this day wasn't embarrassing enough.

We walked back out into the bar. There were a few glances from some of the bikers, but for the most part, no one seemed to notice us, even though the bar was crowded. I was happy to be getting out of there. The sooner I got out, the better.

Talon called over another man. He was older, probably in his sixties, and he looked friendly. At least, he gave me a friendly smile. "Tina, this is Doc," Talon said. "He'll make sure you get home safe tonight."

Doc raised an eyebrow at Talon but then smiled and nodded, clearly accepting his orders. "Pleasure to meet you, Tina," he said.

I smiled hesitantly back. "You too."

We walked outside into the parking lot. I pointed at my car in the back. "That's my car over there," I said. As if it wasn't obvious. There were only a few cars in the entire lot which was mostly overrun by motorcycles. And from the sounds of it, most of the people inside were regulars.

"I'll go get my bike," said Doc. "Don't worry. Whatever trouble you're in, Talon will sort you out. I promise."

I smiled, feeling a little more reassured.

And then, when Talon and I were only a few feet away from my car, it suddenly blew up with a loud *bang* that left my ears ringing.

Talon acted quickly by tackling me to the ground and shielding me from the explosion. There was distant shouting but it barely registered for me. My car just blew up. How was I supposed to get to work?

Talon dragged me to my feet. He was saying something to me, but I couldn't hear it over the ringing. His brow furrowed in concern. Then he put an arm around my shoulders and steered me towards the bar.

Somehow I ended up back in his office with Doc, who had a medical kit. "I'm going to take a quick look at you," he said, his voice calm. "I have to make sure you weren't injured in the blast."

"I'm fine," I said. My voice came out in a monotone. "Talon shielded me. He might be injured."

"I'm okay," said a deep voice beside me. It took me a second to realize it was Talon. He was sitting right next to me on the couch. How did I miss that?

Doc checked the back of my head and asked me a series of questions, which I answered. He flashed a light in my eyes as well. Finally, he was done. "I think you're shaken up and in slight shock," he said. "But no concussion. Are there still shock blankets behind the desk?"

"I'll go get one," Talon said.

"You guys have shock blankets?" Was that standard protocol for biker bars?

"Now and then we do raids of the Demon biker gang compounds," Doc said. "We don't go as often as the other chapters because we're a little more removed from the action, but when we do, shock blankets come in handy for us and the people we rescue."

I looked from him to Talon who was handing me a blanket. "Oh," I said dumbly. I couldn't think of anything else to say.

"Wrap it around you and rest for a little while," Doc said. "You'll be fine." He smiled kindly at me before standing up.

I wrapped the blanket around my shoulders. I had been dreaming about snuggling into a blanket all day but this wasn't what I had in mind.

Doc left the office, leaving just me and Talon left. He handed me the stuffy, his expression conflicted. I hugged it to my chest, under the blanket. "I'll be right back," he said. "Just hang tight. I promise I'll help you get through this."

4

Talon

I left the office to find Doc. "What do you think?" I asked. "Do you think it was the Demons?"

Doc nodded. "There's been no talk of a new player in town, especially one with the resources and stupidity to blow up a car on our property."

I grimaced. That never would have happened under Hawk's leadership. The Demon biker gang had enough run-ins with Hawk to know better than to mess with him. "I want them hit and hit hard," I said. "It's about time they know their place around here."

Doc nodded. "Absolutely. But maybe you should get the lady settled in first. I don't think she should go home. Not alone at least."

He was right. I wouldn't be surprised if they attacked her home as well. All because her old man owed them money. Pieces of shit.

"Shit," I said, rubbing the back of my neck. "Would you be able to take her?"

Doc shook his head. "I'm having renovations done on my house all week. My place is a mess."

I grimaced. "Axel can't leave until past midnight tonight. And he's going to have to collect some debts tomorrow. Maybe I can ask someone else–"

"Why doesn't she just stay with you?" Doc asked, raising an eyebrow.

I sighed. I knew it was the logical choice, but that was playing a dangerous game. She already set off my Daddy instincts. Having her so close to me would just make it worse. But I knew I needed to do something. I couldn't just leave her to go home and potentially get hurt.

I would have to take her in and somehow try to keep things professional.

I went back into the office. Tina was looking a little better and relaxed. She was still clutching the blanket around her with the stuffy against her chest. She looked up at me with wide eyes. "I don't have a ride to work tomorrow," she said.

"I don't think you should go to work tomorrow. They know where you work, and they probably know where you live. Hell, they might have been watching you for awhile before they approached you. Maybe even to give your father extra incentive to make payments."

She snorted and looked away. "I doubt that," she said. "Those incentives wouldn't work. My father never cared about me. He kicked me out of the house when I was fifteen years old."

I frowned. "Jesus. How did you survive?"

She shrugged. "I got an afterschool job and a babysitting job. I stayed over at friends' houses when I had the option. I stayed in a homeless shelter that didn't ask to many questions the rest of the time. I made do and scraped enough earnings together to eventually get an apartment. I've been trying to get by ever since."

My chest tightened when I listened to her story. It was unfortunately not uncommon, especially in these parts. But it was painful to hear anyway. I was just glad she grew up in this town and not a town like Newbury or Middleton, which the Demons used as hunting grounds for their brothels. She would have been snatched up in an instant.

I cleared my throat and tried to keep my expression neutral. I had to remained professional and unattached. I couldn't let her know how proactive I was slowly becoming of her. "I still think there's a good chance they know where you live," I said. "I want you to stay the night at my place. I have a guest room you can use and you'll be safe there. I promise."

She bit her lip, looking hesitant. "I-I'm not sure. No offense but I barely know you."

I nodded. "I understand. But if the Demons are after you, then you need to be under protection. I could come to your place if that makes you feel better."

She shook her head. "That won't work. I only have a studio apartment. I-- I can stay at your place." She stood up and put the blanket down. "I feel a lot better. Tell Doc I said thanks."

"I will." I surveyed her critically. Her waitressing outfit

was slightly skimpy with the short skirt and the bare arms. She would be freezing on my bike in just that. I quickly shed my jacket and handed it to her. "Here," I said. "You'll be warmer in this."

She took the jacket hesitantly. As she did, her eyes traveled over my muscled arms. I couldn't tell if she was looking at the scars or the tattoos that covered them, but a slow blush crept over her face. Fuck. As scared as she was, she was also attracted to me. A part of me enjoyed that. But I pushed that impulse away. I couldn't think about that. Not at all.

Tina put the jacket on and zipped it up. On her, it fell to the middle of her thighs. She was practically swimming in it. But she looked adorable and at least she would be warm.

We left the office. I met eyes with Axel, who was manning the bar. He nodded at me, knowing I would have to take Tina back to my place. I couldn't help but feel some frustration knowing I would have a lot of work I would need to get done tomorrow, and I felt a little guilty for leaving so early in the night. But I wasn't about to make Tina, who was clearly exhausted, just wait in my office all night. I needed to get her home and in bed.

We went outside to my bike. I handed her my helmet. "Put this on," I said. "Have you ever ridden on a motorcycle before?"

She shook her head. "Never." Her eyes were wide with a mixture of fear and excitement.

I smiled. "It's okay," I said. "I'll go slow, I promise." I got on the motorcycle and told her to get on behind me.

As she did, she wrapped her arms around my waist and her tiny body was pressed against my back. Fuck, she felt good.

Slowly, I pulled out of the parking lot and went down the road. I kept my eyes out for someone tailing us, but I couldn't see anyone at all. But it was late now, and I wasn't as experienced as detecting a tail as Hawk was.

Why the hell did he ever make me president? Did I really have what it took to run the Hell's Renegades?

After tonight, I really wasn't sure.

I was going so slow, it took almost an hour to rock up to my home. I lived in a small house near the edge of town. It was a bare bones kind of place, with no frills on the outside, just a weed-filled lawn and a stone pathway leaving up to the door. No flower beds or cheerful shutters. Not even a welcome mat. Tonight was the first time it bothered me. I wish I had a warmer, more welcoming place to bring Tina home to. She deserved comfort, especially after the day she had. Not that she would ever feel comfort with someone like me.

5

Tina

I followed Talon inside his home, feeling more than a little nervous. This wasn't any more dangerous than going to the homeless shelter as a teenager. Or at least, that's what I told myself. But inside these walls, he was in complete control. He could trap me and use me for his own pleasure if he wanted to. The thought filled me with terror but also a small shiver of excitement.

Talon turned on a light to reveal the interior of the house. It held minimal comfort. The living room just had a couch and a TV, but no throw blankets or pictures on the wall. There wasn't even a rug to cushion the hardwood floor. He led me down a barren hallway to bedrooms. He opened one to reveal a queen-sized bed covered in a comforter. It was next to a nightstand with a lamp, but there wasn't anything else in the room. Talon's house reminded me of him-- cold and unattached.

"My room is across the hall and the bathroom is next to your room," Talon said. He wasn't looking at me. He was looking at a spot on the wall past my right shoulder. I couldn't tell if he felt awkward or just annoyed he had to open up his home to me. "You can help yourself to anything in the closet. And your door locks from the inside if it makes you feel more comfortable."

"Thank you," I said. "And thank you for letting me stay here. I promise I won't be too much trouble. I'll be quiet. And clean up after myself." I just hoped his place wouldn't get blown up like my car did.

Finally, his eyes met mine. "Don't worry about that," he said. "Really. I don't have guests often, but I like your company. And I would rather have you here than in even more danger. I don't want you to worry about me kicking you out suddenly because you put your shoes in the wrong place or something."

I felt a lump form in my throat. Because as much as I didn't want to admit it, I was worried about exactly that. If he kicked me out, then I would be stranded and completely vulnerable, just like when I was fifteen. So I felt a little better with his words.

On impulse, I reached out to hug him. He tensed up as my arms went out his waist, but he recovered enough to put an arm around my shoulder. I stepped back. "I'm sorry," I said. "I really wanted to do that. It's been a rough day, but you've made it better."

He gave me a strained smile as he took a step back. "I get it," he said. "You've been through hell. I hope you sleep well."

He left without another word. I felt a little weird from the hug, but it was an impulse from being exhausted. So far Talon was the main thing keeping me away from that awful man from earlier and I had just wanted to hug him. I would have to apologize to him in the morning.

After locking the door, I undressed, folding my clothes up neatly and putting them on the nightstand. It still wouldn't hurt to be as neat as possible, even if Talon said he won't kick me out.

Remembering what he said about the closet, I opened it up. There wasn't much in there, just some old clothes hanging up. I grabbed a t-shirt that was so big, it would practically be a nightgown on me. And in the corner of the closet, in a small basket, were a bunch of stuffies. I stared at them. Why would Talon have these here? There wasn't any evidence he had a kid or anything.

I bit my lip. He probably forgot about the stuffies in there and only meant I could use the clothes. But I wanted to curl up with a stuffy. I couldn't be hurting anything just cuddling with one, right?

I grabbed a small teddy bear and hugged it to my chest. Just holding a stuffy made me feel immediately better.

I shut the closet door and went to bed dressed in one of Talon's old t-shirts and holding a teddy bear. As soon as I was under the covers with the teddy, I was asleep.

The next day, I woke up to the smell of coffee and the sound of bacon sizzling. I groaned, thinking I was still dreaming. I had to be dreaming about the diner, right? There was no way this could be real. Right?

I stood up and slowly padded to the kitchen. Talon was at the stove, cooking. He tensed up and spun around when I entered. I shrank back a little. "I'm sorry," I said automatically.

"No, no I'm sorry," he said, his expression immediately softening. "I didn't mean to scare you. I'm... I'm just not used to having guests. Did you sleep all right? I see you found the closet. That's good." He nodded to the teddy bear I was still holding.

I bit my lip. "Yes, thank you," I said, sitting down at the kitchen table.

He turned back to the stove. "I hope you liked eggs and bacon," he said. "I should have asked what you prefer for breakfast, but I didn't want to wake you."

"Eggs and bacon are fine," I said. "Can I ask you something?"

"It depends."

"Why... why are there so many stuffies around here and at Hawk's Landing?"

6

Talon

I knew the question was coming but I still didn't know how to answer it. I could have kept it a secret and told her not to go into the closet. But I didn't want to deny her comfort, especially when she had gone through hell.

But how was I supposed to tell her I was a Daddy while staying unattached?

"Because the bikers of Hell's Renegades and I.... we're Daddies. We like our old ladies to be Littles-- like you."

She blushed beet red and I knew she knew exactly what I was talking about. The fact that she already knew she was a Little made this easier. "All of you are Daddies?"

"More or less," I said. "We didn't know it when the club formed, but as more of us took old ladies, it became clear there was a pattern. The stuffy in my office belongs to Ramona. She's the old lady of the former club president.

I've only been there a week, so the office looks about the same as it did when Hawk was president."

"And the stuffies in your closet?"

"Those are for any Littles I take." I turned back to the food. "But you don't have to worry. I'm not going to be taking on anymore Littles. Not for a long time at least."

"Why not?"

I focused on plating the food. I kept an image of her terrified face in my mind. She was terrified of me. I had to remember that. It was the only thing that I would keep me from going back on the oath I made myself. "Because I'm club president. As long as I'm president, I have a target on my back. And if I take a Little, then they will be in constant danger too."

I put a plate of food in front of her. "Here," I said. "Enjoy."

She started to pick up a piece of bacon, but she was still looking at me curiously. "But didn't you say the former president had a Little?"

"Yes, and he retired so he could spend more time with her. Besides, Hawk was better at protecting her. He was good at protecting all of us. I'm barely able to run the bar right now."

"It sounds lonely," she said.

I shrugged. "As long as it keeps people safe, then it's for the best." I turned away. "After breakfast, I want you to call out of work. I want you with me at Hawk's Landing until we straighten out the Demons."

She bit her lip. "How long do you think that will take?"

"I'm going to work on it today," I said. "Soon you'll be back to your normal life, just like usual."

Tina gave a hesitant smile as she hugged the teddy bear tighter to her chest. "Thank you." Her Little voice slipped out. God it sounded so sweet.

"Don't mention it," I said.

An hour later, we were ready to go the bar. Tina was dressed in her diner uniform again and I realized she had no other clothes. We would have to make a pit stop first.

We biked through town to the first clothing store I found. We rocked up to the entrance.

"Why are we stopping?" Tina asked.

"Because you need a change of clothes. I'm not going to make you wear your uniform all day."

Panic flickered across her face. "I don't have any money," she said. "My wallet got burned up with my car."

"It's okay. It's on me."

"But--"

"No. You don't get to argue with me on this. Understand?" I raised my eyebrow, giving her my best Daddy expression. Was it fair? No. But I wasn't about to let her spend the entire day in a dirty waitressing uniform that left her arms and legs mostly bare.

She looked down, a small flush rising to her cheeks. "Yes, D... yes." she said meekly.

Fuck. She had almost called me Daddy. And it would have been amazing hearing her say that. "Let's go," I said, my voice a little hoarse with need.

We went into the store and she immediately went to the sales rack. I wanted to tell her to get anything she wanted and that it didn't have to be cheap. But I didn't know how. Not without sounding like a Daddy again.

She ended up picking out a cute pink dress. "Is this okay?" she asked, holding up the dress.

It was a pink dress trimmed in lace and with a heart shaped pocket on the skirt. She would look absolutely adorable in it and it was at least longer than her waitressing uniform. I nodded. "It's perfect. But you'll have to wear my jacket, okay? I don't want you getting cold."

She smiled softly. "That's okay. I like wearing your jacket. It's comfortable." She blushed and went to go stand in line.

Fuck. She was going to be the death of me.

7

Tina

As soon as we checked out, Talon had me change into the dress. I felt instantly better. I never felt comfortable in jeans but this dress was soft and comfortable and I didn't feel nearly as exposed as I did in my waitressing uniform. I was glad he let me get it. I was a little worried he wouldn't want me to wear something that was obviously a Little dress, especially when it might give the other bikers the wrong impression. But he seemed okay with it. If I didn't know any better, I would say he even enjoyed me wearing it.

As soon as I left the bathroom, Talon was watching me. His gaze heated up when he saw me but his expression was neutral the next second. He handed me his jacket without a word.

I looked at him, in only a t-shirt. "Won't you be cold?" I asked.

"I'll be fine. I promise. I just want you to be warm."

I smiled. "Thank you," I said shyly.

"Don't mention it."

I wrapped up in his jacket, feeling even better and more protected. As we went outside, I stopped suddenly. There were a couple of guys hanging out around Talon's bike. And one of them was the man who had tried to kidnap me outside of work.

I tugged on Talon's hand. "That's him," I whispered, staring at the strange man. "That's the guy who my father owed."

Talon followed my gaze and his mouth twisted into a sneer. "Reaper," he said. "He's one of the highest-ranking people in the Demon biker gang. Go back inside. I'll take care of this. I promise."

"I don't want you to get hurt because of me."

He looked at me. With a scowl on his face, he looked terrifying. Even though I knew he would never hurt me and he wasn't even angry at me, it took all of my willpower not to take a step back. "I won't let you get hurt, baby girl. Now do as your told. Wait inside until this is over."

I swallowed. "Yes, Daddy." I couldn't help it. In this moment, there was nothing else I could possibly call him.

I went inside the store and I watched him approach the group of men. I looked around. No one else was in the store. It was empty aside from a man behind the cash register. He was bored and looking through his phone.

I looked back outside. I could barely hear what they were saying.

"You're more stupid than I thought, Reaper," Talon was saying. "Blowing up a vehicle at Hawk's Landing is asking for trouble."

"Maybe when Hawk was still around," Reaper said. "I'm not afraid of you. You're nothing."

Talon laughed, but it was a cold laugh without humor. "You had better get out of here while I'm still feeling generous."

"No," Reaper said. "I don't think I will." He and his men surrounded Talon. "It's time to teach you a lesson. And then I'm going to take what's mine and I'm going to enjoy breaking her in."

Talon threw the first punch, hitting Reaper in the nose. Reaper's men grabbed a hold of Talon, one for each arm. He managed to get one arm free and punch another in the nose, but then Reaper punched him in the stomach.

The fight continued and Talon managed to hold his own for awhile, but he was up against three men and it wasn't long before he was on the ground and Reaper was punching him in the face. I felt sick to my stomach. I couldn't let him get killed over this but that was exactly what Reaper was going to do.

Before I could stop myself, I ran out of the store. "Stop!" I shouted. "Please, stop."

Reaper paused and grinned at the sight of me. "Well, don't you look cute. Talon sweet on you or something? Dressing you up like a doll like that?"

"Let him go," I said. "Please. I'll go with you. I'll do whatever you say. But you have to let him go now."

Reaper pretended to think it over. "I could," he said. "Or I could just kill him and take you anyway."

"Then I'll scream fire," I said. "And everyone inside that store will hear me and someone will call the cops. You think I won't? People inside are already noticing the fight. Do you really want to stick around for the cops to come? Or more Hell's Renegades? They'll be on their way too, you know they will. If you let him go, I'll go with you right now." I was talking fast, trying to say everything I could think of to persuade Reaper to let Talon go.

Talon looked up at me from the ground. His face was bloody, so bloody I couldn't even tell where it was coming from. "Tina," he said, coughing. "Don't. Run. Please."

I shook my head silently.

Reaper finally nodded. He signaled his men to fall back and he grabbed my arm. I felt bile rise up in my throat as I went with him. But it was worth it if Talon got out of this alive.

I forced myself to take deep breaths as Reaper dragged me to his motorcycle. Talon would get reinforcements and he would come for me. I had to believe that.

8

Talon

I barely picked myself off the ground. My entire body was screaming at me to stop. Everything hurt so much but I needed to call someone. Anyone. I needed them to go after Reaper, whose bike was disappearing in the distance with Tina on it.

Coughing, I dialed the first number I could think off. Hawk picked up immediately. "What's up?"

"She's gone," I said, coughing. "I couldn't protect her."

"The woman from the bar?"

"Yeah. Reaper was after her and he got her."

"Where are you now?"

I told him where I was and he hung up. I knew he was going to come after me, but I needed people to go after Tina and Reaper. I sat down on my bike. My head was spinning. I dialed Axel's number next. He picked up after a couple of rings. "Hello?" he asked. It sounded like he had just woken up.

"How soon can you get a few bikers together?" I asked.

He was immediately awake. "Give me fifteen minutes. Why? What happened?"

"Reaper took Tina. They were headed towards Middleton. I need you to get some people to go after them."

"Are you okay? You sound like shit."

I wiped some blood out of my eyes. "I'll be fine," I said. "There were three of them and one of me. I broke Reaper's nose, though."

Axel swore. "They're going to have to pay," he said. "They can't just go after our president like that."

"We'll worry about retaliation later," I said. "Right now, all I care about is getting Tina." If they were too late... if she was already hurt... I felt like I was going to throw up and not just from the injuries.

"I'm going, I'm going," he said. "I'll get Doc and a few other guys together. I'll meet you back at the bar later."

"Thanks," I said weakly before hanging up.

My vision started to spin. I was barely aware when a bike pulled up next to mine. I looked up to see Hawk getting off of it with Ramona, who had a first aid kit.

"Jesus," Hawk said. "They fucked you up good."

Ramona quickly opened up the kit and pulled out some gauze. She started mopping up my face. "You need to go to the hospital," she said.

"I can't," I said. "I'm not going until Tina is back."

"I should have known better than to choose a stubborn son of a bitch to replace me," said Hawk."

"As if you would have chosen anyone else," said Ramona. "Can you please get him some water?

Hawk pulled a bottle of water out of his jacket pocket and handed it to me. "Drink."

I took a long drink. The water cleared my head a little. "I sent Axel after Tina and Reaper."

"I know," said Hawk. "That's what I would have done." He gave me a half smile as he handed me some ibuprofen. I swallowed it down with more water.

Most of the blood came from my nose and the corner of my right eye, but Ramona cleaned and bandaged a cut over my left eyebrow before giving me a cold pack to keep down the swelling on my eyes. "You almost definitely have a concussion," she said. "I can't patch you up as good as Doc, but you'll live."

"Thank you," I said. "I'm sorry I pulled you two into this."

Ramona grinned. "Oh, I'm used to it," she said. "I knew he wouldn't be able to walk away from the club completely and I never expected him to." She gave Hawk a goofy grin. He smiled in return. It was strange seeing him look so relaxed and happy. I felt a twinge of envy at seeing the two of them so happy together.

"I don't think I'm cut out to be president," I said. "Club members might respect me, but the Demons think they can pull any shit they want. They blew up a car at the bar and they took Tina right in front of me. I can't do this."

"They'll learn to fear you," Hawk said. "Just like they did me. You think I could take three guys at once?"

I gave a slight grin. "I don't know. You sure act like it sometimes."

He grinned. "Maybe. But that's all that is. They might not respect you now, but that'll change. You'll show them. But first you need to wait to see out of both of your eyes."

"You're right about that."

"Let's get you back to the bar. Ramona will bike you back."

I nodded in agreement, knowing Hawk taught his Little well on the bike. Right now, she probably knew how to bike better than I did.

Ramona and I followed Hawk back to the bar. We rocked up to it. There smoking remains of the explosion was still outside, but it looked like some effort to move the debris out of the way was made. I would have to collect all the debris and lug it to a disposal site. Just another thing to add to the list.

The bar was empty and dark inside. I slumped into one of the seats. Part of me wanted to go to sleep, but most of me was anxious and restless. I needed to hear news about Tina. The sooner the better.

"I'll go get some more water," said Ramona. "And maybe some coffee as well."

"Thanks, baby girl," Hawk said, kissing her on the forehead.

Ramona smiled, leaning into her Daddy's touch before disappearing into the kitchen.

"I don't know how you did it, man," I said. "How the hell did you run the club, get an old lady, and make it out of here alive."

Hawk gave me a crooked grin. "It wasn't easy," he said. "Honestly, I don't think I would have lasted so long without Ramona. She kept me sane. If it wasn't for her, I would have taken bigger risks. I would have gotten more careless. And I would have ended up getting myself killed years ago."

"Didn't you worry about putting her in danger?"

His smile disappeared. "Every day," he said. "There were a few close calls, too. It scared the absolute shit out of me. But I gave her the choice to leave. I would have been happy to support her and make sure she was cared for, even if she never wanted to see me again. But she wanted to stay. And I'm glad she did." He raised an eyebrow at me. "Are you sweet on Tina? You're asking a lot of questions all of a sudden."

"I might be," I admitted. "Not that it matters now. I doubt she would want me when I can't even protect her."

"You just sent a small army after her," Hawk said. "You think Axel would rally up less than twenty bikers for this mission?"

"Fair point." I sighed. "I don't know. I don't like the idea of putting Tina in danger. She's been through hell. Even before all of this shit with the Demons."

"Look, we might be Daddies and take a dominant role with Littles, but in the end, it's up to them on staying or leaving," Talon said. "And if she wants to stay, there's nothing you can do that will make you change her mind."

Part of me wanted that. I wanted her to be my Little. And a selfish part of me hoped she wanted me as a Daddy. But none of it would matter if she didn't return safely.

9

Tina

Reaper biked fast, a lot faster than Talon ever did. I had been hoping I would have a chance to let go and run into the woods where they couldn't follow me, but that wasn't possible. I had to cling to him for dear life and I hated every second of it.

But Reaper seemed to be biking fast, even swerving in between cars and flying around corners. It was almost like he was running for something.

Maybe he was more scared of Talon than he let on.

I just hoped they would catch up to us before we reached our destination. But judging by this pace, I doubted it.

I felt a heavy pit in my stomach when we pulled up to what looked like a warehouse surrounded by a barbed wire fence. The gate swung open for us and Reaper sped in, his lackeys right behind us.

As soon as we were inside, he skidded to a stop. I felt so nauseous from the fast ride, I immediately doubled over and heaved. Reaper gripped my arm and pulled me to my feet. "You're not going to get out of this that easily," he said. "We both know you rode bitch on Talon's bike without any problem. You're not going to get sick on mine."

I took deep breaths and straightened up, glaring at him. "I came with you willingly, didn't I? You don't have to manhandle me."

He grinned and his two lackeys started laughing behind me. "You're going to have to get used to getting manhandled, sweetheart," Reaper said. "How else do you think you'll pay your father's debt."

I swallowed. *Please, Talon. Please find me now.* I wasn't expecting him in person, after the beating he took, but I knew he would send men after me. He wouldn't just let me get tortured by the Reaper.

"Get her inside and throw her into a room," Reaper said. "We'll break her in soon but first I want to make sure we weren't followed."

The two men grabbed my arms and dragged me inside the warehouse. We went down a long, decrepit looking hall. The building looked like it was falling apart from the inside out. I doubted this was really their base of operations. Probably just a hideout to stay away from the Hell's Renegades and the cops. A place to beat their victims into submission.

They opened up a door that practically screamed on its hinges before throwing me into a dusty, empty room.

One of the men grinned and knelt down on the ground next to me. I shrank away from him but there wasn't any place for me to run. "I'm going to have so much fun breaking in a cute little thing like you," he said. He slid a hand up my thigh, underneath my skirt. My skin crawled.

"Come on, man, we got to go. Reaper's orders," the other man said. "You can play with the new toy later."

The man sighed and removed his hand before standing up. "Enjoy the peace and quiet," he told me. "It's the last peace and quiet you'll ever have."

I knew he was right. Unless I got out of here. And I couldn't wait on the Hell's Renegades to make that happen.

The door swung shut behind them, leaving me alone. I got to my feet and started looking around. The room was dimly lit and empty. A thick layer of dust covered everything, making it hard to breathe.

I started trailing my hands along the wall, looking for a light switch. But when I found it, it didn't work.

The only light was coming from a window that was covered in dust and cobwebs. There wasn't anything in the room I could use to break it, but maybe I could pry it open somehow.

The windowpane was locked into place. It felt a lot like the window locks that my childhood home had. I grabbed at the lock and tried to open it, but it was rusted shut. I grunted and pulled until my fingers were raw but it barely budged.

I turned to the door. There was no way they would just

leave it open, right? And even if they did, those hinges were loud. Someone might hear…

But it was the only chance I had. If I stayed in this room then I was as good as dead. I tried the doorknob. It was locked. But like everything else in this place, the door was falling apart. Maybe, if I put enough force on it, I would be able to bust the door off.

I shoved at the door and it didn't budge. Then I leaned all of my weight against the door and the lock gave way a little. The drywall around it started to crumble and I felt a flicker of hope. I backed up a couple of steps and threw myself against the door. The drywall gave way and the door swung open, the hinges squealing with the movement. I stumbled out of the room and didn't give myself time to catch my breath. I started running for the entrance.

I knew it was probably stupid to go through the front entrance, but I didn't know if anyone else was in the building or who heard the door. I could only hope I could leave out of the only exit I knew.

I ran to the door and my stomach flipped over with relief as it opened and I was breathing fresh air again. I looked around, but no one was around. It looked like the place had cleared out to make sure the Hell's Renegades weren't following me. It was clear no one expected I would find a way out of that room by myself.

The gate was locked. I looked up the chain link fence and grimaced. At the top was barbed wire. I could probably get over, but not without scratching myself up. However, I didn't see much of an option right now.

I climbed up the fence and to the barbed wire. Taking a deep breath, I grabbed onto the wire, wincing as the barbs poked and scratched at my skin. Bunching my skirt up, I managed to hook a leg over the wire. A barb cut deep in my leg, leaving a long, deep scratch that brought tears to my eyes. I forced myself to keep going.

Carefully, I managed to pull myself over the barbed wire and I dropped to the other side, landing on my knees. Pain radiated throughout my legs and I groaned.

I managed to get to my feet and limped slowly across the street, to the forest on the other side. From there, I started to follow the road away from the warehouse, but I stayed hidden in the trees, knowing someone could discover my absence at any time.

A roar of motorcycles came in the distance and I fell to the ground as they rounded the corner. I stayed still, even as one skidded to a stop. Lying on the ground, I didn't dare move an inch. I didn't even breathe.

The biker who stopped looked in my direction, as if he was studying the trees. Then he slowly got off his bike and walked toward me.

Shit. He saw me. I stood up and tried to run, but with my hurt leg, I wasn't running fast. The biker caught up to me in a matter of seconds and he grabbed my arm.

I spun around, ready to fight, but he caught my hand before I could hit him. "Tina?" he said, flipping back the visor of his motorcycle helmet.

I could have cried with relief. "Doc?"

He pulled me into a brief hug before he looked me up

and down. "You look like you tried to wrestle a mountain lion."

"Try a barbed wire fence."

He winced. "You're tough, I'll give you that. Let's get you back to the bar before Talon tries to hunt you down himself."

"How is he? Have you seen him?"

"Not yet. Axel said he was in rough shape but his only priority was finding you."

A lump formed in my throat. "It was really bad, Doc. There were three of them and he held them off the best he could but he was barely conscious the last time I saw him."

"I know." Doc put my arm around his shoulders to better support my weight as he walked me to his bike. "There's no way he would have let you go if he was capable of walking."

10

Talon

I don't know how, but somehow I managed to fall asleep on the couch in the office. The next thing I knew, I was being shaken awake.

"Talon, she's here, and she's with Doc," Hawk said.

I got up immediately and groaned when my head started pounding. Slow movements. I was going to have to go slow, even when I didn't want to.

I stumbled out to the bar to see Tina perched on a table while Doc bandaged up a long cut on her leg. Her dress was filthy and a little torn and she looked disheveled, but she was alive. "Are you okay?" I asked, going towards her. "Did they hurt you?"

She shook her head. "No, they never got a chance. Are you okay?"

"I'm fine, don't worry about me. How did your leg get cut like that?"

Doc spoke up. "Barbed wire fence," he said. "She escaped before we even got to the warehouse– Axel is probably blowing it up right now as we speak. You have a tough little lady, Talon."

I smiled softly as I looked down at her. "I do, don't I?"

She smiled back at me and then frowned. "What about you?" she asked. "Are you okay? You should sit down."

"I'm fine, baby girl," I said. "I had a long rest, and I feel better." Well, technically, I felt better. The pounding in my head wasn't great but at least the room wasn't spinning.

"You slept? What if you had a concussion?"

"Common misconception," Doc said. "You can sleep just fine with a concussion." He shot me a stern look. "I'm still looking you over. You might have gotten patched up fine, but I'm checking you out for my own peace of mind."

I nodded. I didn't expect anything less.

Hawk leaned back and crossed his arms. "Looks like you have everything under control," he said. "Ramona and I are going to head out. We have lunch reservations and I don't want to miss them. It's nice to meet you, Tina. I'm glad you're okay."

She nodded and Hawk left. This time I didn't feel helpless seeing him go. He believed I could take care of it all. So it had to be true, right?

Tina leaned against me. "I'm okay, Daddy," she whispered in my ear. "It's all okay."

I closed my eyes, smiling. It felt nice just to hold her and know that she was safe.

The next month was hectic and boring all at once. I

spent most of it trying to run the club while healing. Luckily I had help. Tina quit her job at the diner and came to Hawk's Landing to manage the bar. She said she felt safer at the bar than where she had gotten attacked for the first time. I was grateful for the help.

She also stayed at my place, but even though she wanted to take care of me and make sure I was all right, I insisted she focused on healing herself. I was her Daddy after all. It was my job to take care of her.

Axel blew up the warehouse. And once I felt good enough to get on a bike, I led Hell's Renegade bikers on patrol all through town, looking for Demons to beat the shit out of. It didn't take long for them to crawl out of the woodwork and get out of Dodge.

After a month, things had started to settle down. One morning, I woke up to see Tina bringing me breakfast in bed. I raised an eyebrow as I sat up. "What have I told you about taking care of me, baby girl?"

"I'm all healed, Daddy," she said, twirling around for emphasis. Her puffy skirt flew up, revealing her legs. "See? Not even a scar."

"It's my job to take care of you, baby girl."

She crawled into bed next to me and put her arms around my waist. I was finally healed enough so she could touch me without hurting me. "I know. But I like doing nice things for you, Daddy."

"I know, baby girl." I brushed a piece of hair out of her face. "You know, I am getting better and I'm able to do things on my own. You don't have to stay with me if you don't want to. I can set you up somewhere away from here and make sure you're safe and taken care of. It's dangerous with me, baby girl."

"I know. But I want to stay. And you said you wouldn't make me go, right?"

I smiled softly. "I did. And it's true." I leaned down to kiss her forehead. "I'll never kick you out." I had to admit, I was relieved. I wanted her to stay with me. I just wanted her.

She bit her lip as she looked up at me. "Can I kiss you, Daddy?"

"You never have to ask me that, baby girl." I leaned down to kiss her. Her lips felt sweet and wonderful. I groaned as I deepened the kiss, licking her bottom lip. Her mouth opened to let me inside.

I moved so I was pinning her down to the bed. "You feel so good, baby girl," I whispered as I trailed kisses down her neck. She gasped and squirmed with each kiss.

"Please fuck me, Daddy," she begged. "Please."

"Are you sure you're ready for that, baby girl?" I asked. "You don't have to, you know."

"I know. But I want to. Please, Daddy."

I smiled and kissed her again. "Of course, baby girl."

I slid my hand up her thigh, pausing when I felt her diaper underneath her skirt. I grinned. "You're all dressed up for me, aren't you?"

She blushed slightly. "It's comfy, Daddy."

"I'm glad you like it, baby girl." I gently pulled the diaper off of her and tossed it to the side, revealing her bare pussy underneath. I stroked her slit with my finger, feeling how wet she was. She gasped with every movement and a moan escaped her lips. Her hips bucked up and my fingers slid inside her tight hole. "Fuck," I whispered. "You feel so good, baby girl."

"Please, Daddy. I want you inside me so badly. Please."

"Not yet, baby girl." I started to tease her clit with my fingers as I pressed a kiss against her collarbone. "First I want you to come for me."

I continued to torment her until she started to squirm and pant. I flicked and rubbed her clit, feeling her pussy grow wetter with every movement. I knew she wanted me as much as I wanted her. And it was so much fun watching her come apart for me.

Finally, she couldn't take it anymore and she stiffened up before coming all over my hand. She moaned, squeezing her eyes shut.

I smiled. "That was beautiful, baby girl," I whispered.

"Now will you fuck me, Daddy?"

"You're so impatient." I grinned and kissed her forehead. "But yes, I'll fuck you now. You've been such a good girl, after all." I straightened up and took off my underwear, revealing my hard cock underneath. I stroked it a few times as I watched her. Her gaze heated up at the sight of it, her eyes full of lust and need. I positioned it at her entrance and slowly slid in.

Tina's eyes flickered shut and she moaned. I groaned, feeling her pussy stretch around my cock. She felt like absolute heaven. I couldn't believe she was mine. All mine.

I leaned down to kiss her as I thrust into her over and over. I knew I wanted to watch her come again. I wanted to see that beautiful expression as I made her come undone on my cock. I reached between us and started playing with her clit again. A shiver ran through her body in response. "I want you to come for me again," I said. "I want you to come all over my cock. Can you do that for me, baby girl?"

"Yes, Daddy," she whimpered.

"Good girl," I breathed. "Good girl."

I could feel the orgasm building inside of her and suddenly her body stiffened as she came on my cock. I could feel her pussy undulating all around me and the sensation of it was enough to send me over the edge. I let out a groan as I came.

For a few moments, all I could hear was the sounds of us breathing as we recovered from our orgasms. Then I rolled onto my back and reached out and gathered her into my arms. Tina cuddled up against me, looking exhausted. "Are you okay, baby girl?" I asked.

She nodded with a soft smile. "Yes, Daddy," she said. "That felt amazing."

I smiled and closed my eyes. "It was amazing for me too," I said. I held her tight to me. "I love you, baby girl. I'll do everything in my power to protect you. No matter what."

"I love you too, Daddy." She wrapped her arms around my waist. "I'm yours. All yours. No matter what."

Yay! Talon and Tina are now living their happily ever after? Aren't they perfect for each other? What's next in store for the Hell's Renegades? Find out in *Alluring Biker Daddy*.

Lightning Source UK Ltd.
Milton Keynes UK
UKHW021124120622
404294UK00007B/783